HEIRS OF DARKNESS

A PRINCE OF DARKNESS NOVELLA

AMBER THOMA

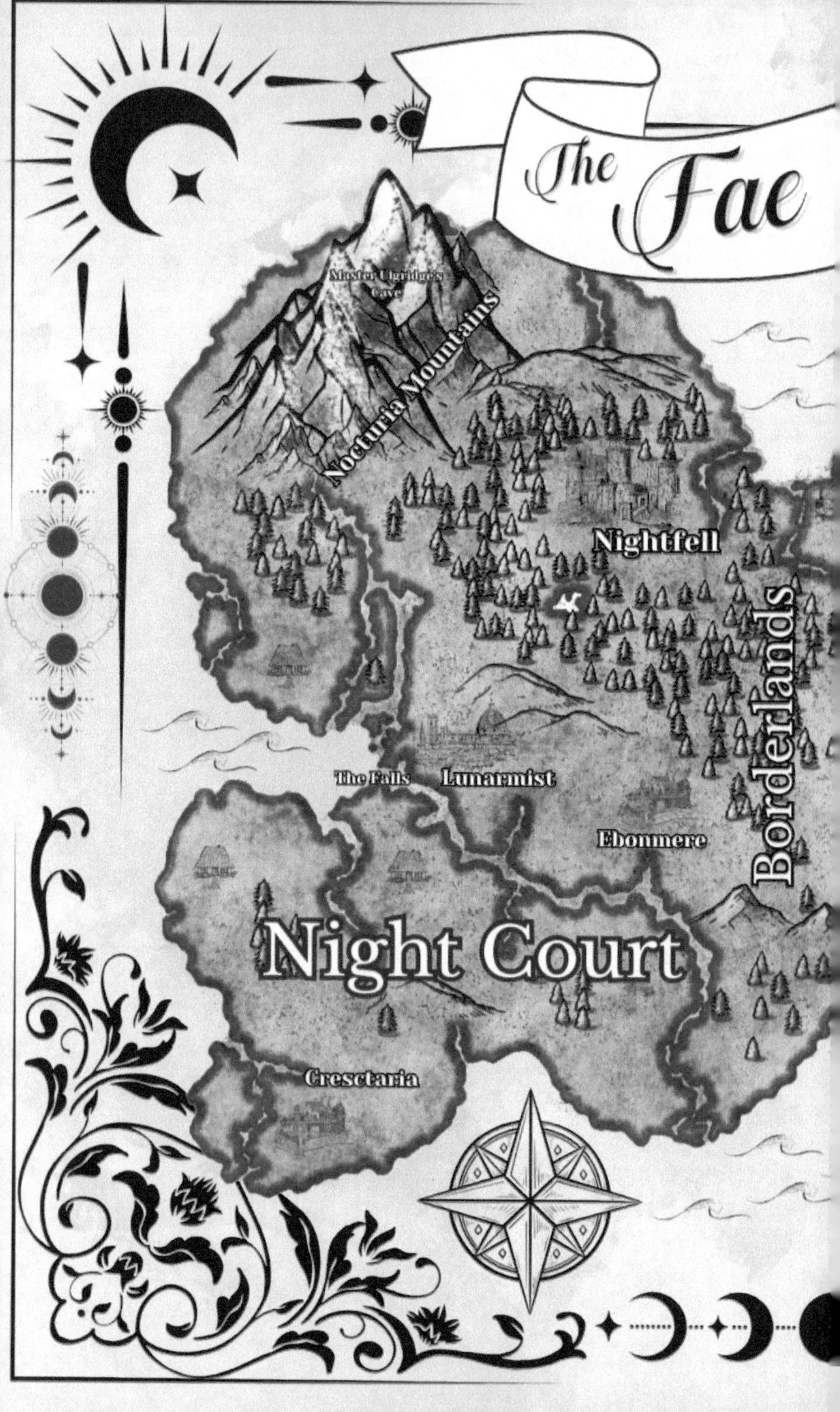

The Fae
Master Upridge's Cave
Nocturia Mountains
Nightfell
Borderlands
The Falls
Lunarmist
Ebonmere
Night Court
Cresctaria

Realm
Solarath
Falling Star Coven
Lunar Crystal Coven
Hallowed Crescent Coven
Daybreak
Day Court
Silver Moon Coven
Mystic Fate Coven
Flarimmar
Coven of Remembrance
Anlu's Village
Temple
Black Cauldron Coven
Southern Day Court

Realms of Lore: Fae Book 1.5

Heirs of Darkness

A Prince of Darkness novella.

Published by: Author Amber Thoma

www.authoramberthoma.com

First Edition Published October 2023

Book Cover by: Rebekah Sinclair

Map and Interior Designs by: Amber Thoma

For all the children who had to fight
to reach adulthood.

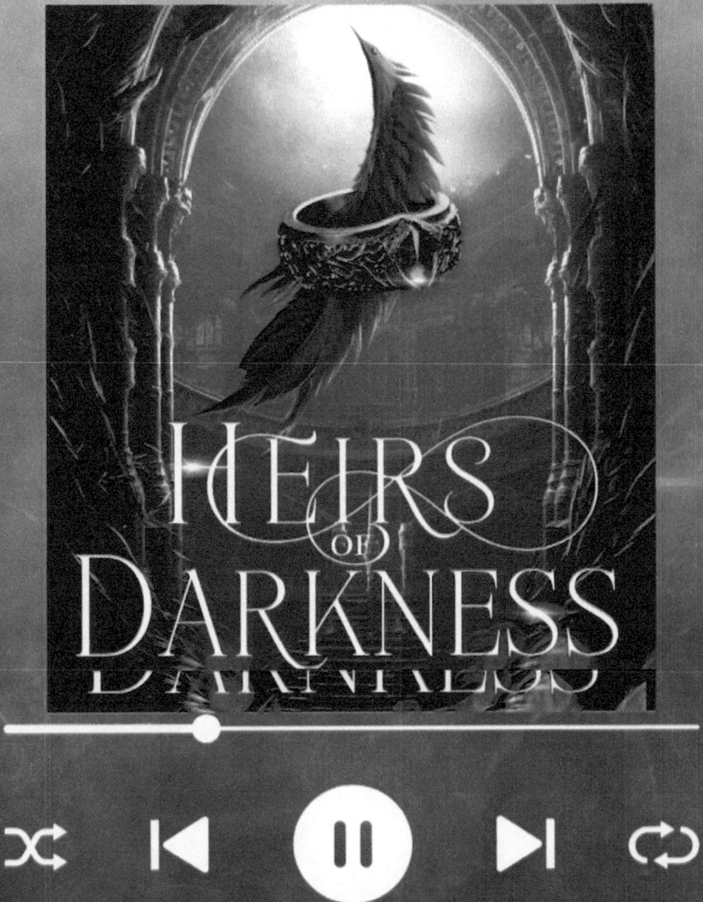

HEIRS
OF
DARKNESS

Dear reader,
I am so happy you decided to read Heirs of Darkness. If you have not read Prince of Darkness yet please STOP now and read that first. Technically, you can read Heirs of Darkness first since this is a prequel, however, for the best reading experience I suggest reading Heirs of Darkness second. If you have already read Prince of Darkness, enjoy your time with our favorite blue giant and feather duster!
Happy reading!

Amber Thoma

Trigger warning: This book contains scenes that may depict, mention, or discuss: abusive relationship, assault, blood, bullying, child abuse, death, emotional abuse, and slavery.

Content Warning: Violence

CONTENTS

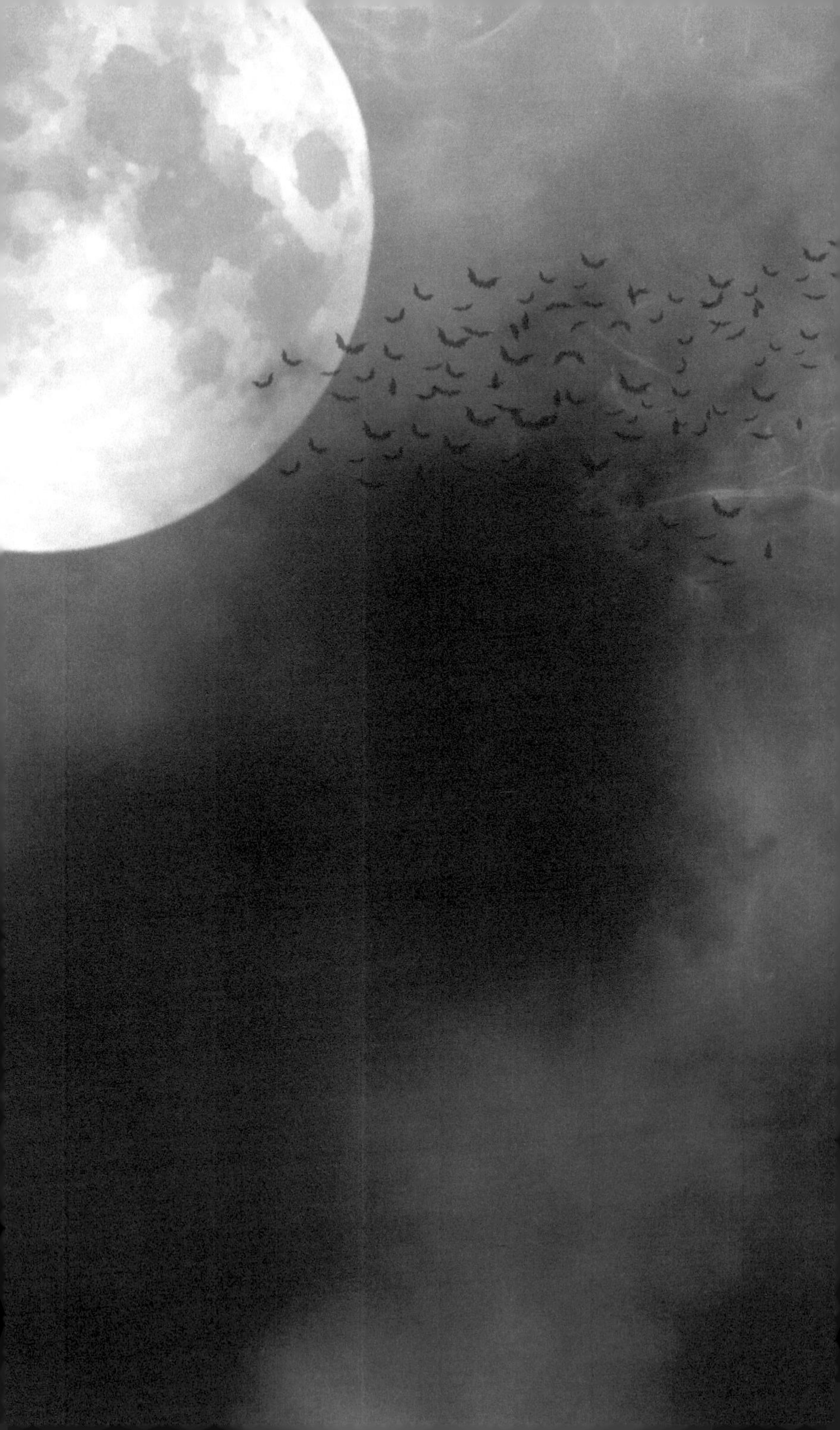

One
Ciaran

9 Years Old

It will not come off.

No matter what I try, the damned thing will not budge. I pull at it for so long and with such force, the fingers I use to grasp it begin to bleed. I am able to twist it, so I try twisting it off. It will not travel down the length of my finger, only moving in a continual circle around and around, tearing my skin the entire time. I try cutting the band, but no blade will pierce it, and no slippery substance will make it slide off.

Having a father like mine, panic was something I had conquered years ago—or so I thought. This ring, however, has created a desperation inside of me that scatters my thoughts and makes it hard to think logically. I can not let him get to me like that ever again.

Last night, when my father presented me with the small box and called it a "gift," I should have been suspicious. He rarely, if ever, gives gifts. Mother sat in her chair next to the fireplace with her customary glass of wine in hand and an empty smile upon her face, making her appear amused while watching us.

Something about her presence always lulls me into a false sense of security. Stupidly, I continue to think she would never let anything too wicked befall me. I will never make that mistake again.

There is no one in the palace I can rely upon, with the exception of my cousin, and my relationship with him is drawing the attention of my father. I have been growing concerned with the frequency with which he mentions the friendship Kes and I share. Now, that concern has morphed into fear.

To my father, any relationship that causes one to care for another is a weakness that needs to be eradicated. Personally, I find that logic baseless. I know Kes will come if I call without question, no matter the circumstances. He would make any of my foes his own. Relationships based on fear create the lack of loyalty I see between my parents, and they both seem miserable.

I allowed myself to become excited over the little box in my father's hand and stood before him within a blink, like any youngling would. My curiosity has always been able to get the better of me, and I enjoy learning the whys and hows of everything I possibly can. I have an insatiable hunger for knowledge, and it seems this time it will be my downfall.

When he opened the box, I was slightly disappointed, because what youngling male cares for shiny bits females like to wear? I tried not to let it show; I was still excited to be given something from my father. He has never been affectionate, and that never bothered me. It's his lack of approval that always digs the deepest, and the gift felt like I had finally earned it.

A small voice in the back of my mind urged caution, but I quickly banished the thought; I am so desperate for his approval. My father's face did nothing to raise any suspicions. I had never seen him look at me in such a way; he was truly pleased. If only I had known it was not directed at me, but at himself. If there had been any other warning signs, his words succeeded in chasing them away.

"I have been holding on to this gift since the day you were born, my son, waiting for the appropriate time to present it to you. While you are still a small youngling, you have gained several years of life experience, setting you on the path to becoming the male I know you will be." His voice held the tone of approval I had been waiting so long to hear, and there was nothing I craved more than to be done with younghood—to finally be a grown male. He knew exactly what to say to lower my guard.

"Thank you, Father. What is it?" I asked him, trying to sound older than my nearly ten years of life.

"This ring gives the one who controls it immense power." I am not surprised the ring has something to do with increasing power. Father is obsessed with gaining as much power as he can, even though everything he does seems to reduce his power year after year.

"Shall I place it upon your finger?" The question sounded innocent enough, and I was too blinded by what I thought would become a cherished memory. I did not notice the gleam of malice in his eyes.

"Yes, Father, of course." Like a fool, I gave him my right hand. When he gently grabbed it, I was filled with a feeling I could not describe. My father had never treated me gently before, and I found this feeling could become addictive. I knew I was grinning from ear to ear, showing off my multitude of teeth.

The very next moment, as my father slid the ring onto my finger, I felt something sharp penetrate the skin beneath and extreme pain flared throughout my body. I felt as though I were on fire and screamed. As soon as the ring was secured on my finger, my father dropped my hand as if it were filthy; he sneered at me as I writhed in pain. I glanced over to my mother, she would surely intervene, but she just looked on with her empty smile and continued to drink the wine from her glass.

Once the burning sensation left, I felt nothing. No power flowed through my veins, and no magic was accessible to me. I could sense it all still lurking within me, but it was as though it had been walled off, preventing me from touching a single drop of it. I felt bereft, as though half of me had been carved away. I could feel tears beginning to form behind my eyes and knew if a single one fell, it would only make matters worse. Father made sure to teach me that lesson early on.

"What? What happened?" I managed to get the words out with as little shaking to my voice as possible.

"I told you, the ring gives immense power to the one that controls it. Did you think I would ever give *you* more power?" He laughed at the confusion I was desperately attempting to keep from my face, but I obviously had not succeeded. "Your stupidity never fails to astound me, boy. The ring gives me access to your power, while also giving me complete control over your body. How else am I ever going to turn you into half the ruler I am?"

I might not have been alive for very long, but from what I have witnessed, my father is a horrible ruler. Instilling fear with public displays of torture to any being, regardless of station, at any time is the only thing he succeeds in. I understand the need for the members of the Night Court to fear their king, but I am still uncertain how it can benefit the court in any way.

My father's words left me speechless. I should not be surprised he was capable of such an act, but I never thought he would steal the power from his own son. My mother continued to stare blankly, showing no alarm over the treatment of her son. It was not until my father's next words that I comprehended what the second part of his gift meant.

"Stand up, boy." I stood, but I had not been the one to tell my body to do so. Dread pooled in my stomach. "Let's go pay a visit to all of those ridiculous places you find so 'wonderful' and 'beautiful' in the woods you were droning on and on about earlier."

Again, my body moved without my control, and we ported to one of my favorite places in the entire forest—the wall of glowing mocking blooms. My father made me rip every single bloom from the wall, while the ones waiting to be touched repeated his commands until only silence remained.

This continued at every place I had excitedly shared with my parents only hours before my father placed the leash around my finger. Every last place I had spent exploring with Kes, I was now leaving a trail of destruction. I vowed to avoid the woods at all costs from that moment on, if only to save the beauty from myself.

I stare at the offending object circling the middle finger of my right hand. It's an unassuming band made from the darkest of red metals. My favorite color. I would think my father did it on purpose if I had any reason to believe he even knows I have a favorite color.

Whenever a human finds themselves in our court, my father displays them in the great hall and tortures them slowly, keeping them alive for as long as possible. The blood pools and dries into the most beautiful color I have ever seen. The only thing my father and I have in common is our love of torture.

Picking up the knife I was using to attempt to cut the band, I resign myself to the only thing I have yet to try—cut the finger off. It will grow back, but the amount of pain is not something I am looking forward to. Before last night, I had not truly experienced pain; the minor slaps and hard grips from my father were nothing compared to the flames that had engulfed my body after the ring pierced my finger.

I take a deep breath, bring the tip of the blade down upon the joint connecting my finger to my hand, and press down. The knife shifts away from the finger as if it were repelled, only to slice into the finger next to it. I must have done something wrong, so I try again with the same results.

I am obviously able to cut myself, just not any part of the finger that would sever the ring from my hand. It must have a spell upon it, protecting the immediate skin around it. I groan as I realize what I will have to do—remove the entire hand.

My palms sweat thinking about how long it will take me to slice through my entire wrist. If my claws were fully grown, I could probably do it in one quick slice, but as they are now, I doubt they can even slice through my smallest finger. Based on the way the knife easily parted the skin on my other fingers, I am hoping it will be sharp enough, but there is only one way to know for certain.

It takes me a few minutes to gather my courage, but eventually I bring the tip of the knife to the center of my wrist, not really sure how to go about this. I gulp down several deep breaths, let out a scream between my teeth, and close my eyes as I shove the blade in until it meets something hard and becomes stuck. It's surprisingly painless.

At least that is what I thought until I notice the tip of the blade is at least an inch deep into the table next to my wrist. No matter how many times I try to cut off my hand, the blade will not strike. I try moving up my arm with the same results, again and again.

I throw the knife across the room, and it buries itself into the side of a dresser. I feel something damp on my face and realize the tears I have been holding in since last night are now free. There is no way for me to remove it, and somehow I have to come to terms with this knowledge. The tears were of pain last night, but now they are of frustration.

Logically, I know I have no means to rid myself of this ring, but my mind refuses to accept relinquishing control of my body to anyone, let alone my father. A thought crosses my mind that has me going unnaturally still.

Kes. He will make me harm Kes.

The only thing I have any control over is making sure my father thinks I have grown tired of my attachment to my cousin. I will push him away and avoid him whenever I can, and if my father is around, I will make it seem as though I detest Kes. I cannot see another way to protect him than to stay away—just like the woods.

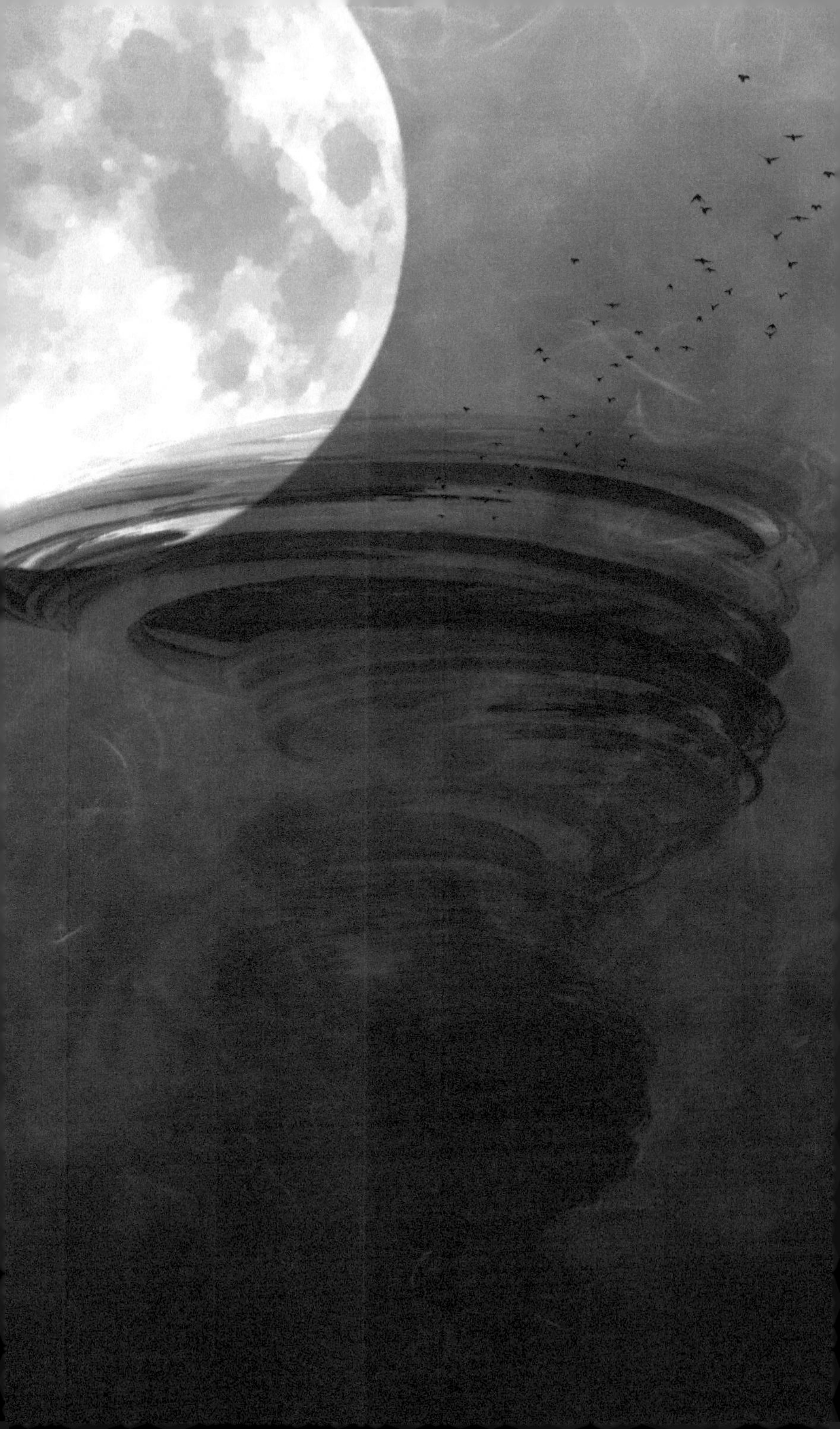

Two
KES

"Ciaran!" I call to my cousin from down the hall. He does not even turn to look as he walks on. I am not exactly surprised. His behavior has been strange over the past several months. There have been times he would be doing any mundane action and stop in the middle of whatever it was, walk away stiffly, and leave his things behind. His walking is another strange behavior. I have not seen him port *once* since the last time we went to the woods. With our wings not large enough for us to fly, it's even stranger to see him not use it.

From the second we learned to port, we started popping up all over the palace and realm, seeing what trouble we could get into. Now, he seems to be following his father around like a little puppy, which is also strange. We used to laugh at the stupid things his father would say while we tried to imitate his voice; now the two were never far apart.

It does not make sense. The shadows that once followed him everywhere, a swirling mass of all consuming darkness, are suddenly gone. He seems like a lesser fae—powerless.

The change in my cousin has been sudden. For weeks, I thought he could not hear me, or was dealing with another one of the missions his father often gave him to "prove himself worthy" of the throne. After months of being ignored, I realized *that* was exactly what he was doing—ignoring me.

The adjustment has not been an easy one; being a youngling in the Nightfell Palace alone is not a kind life. It does not seem to matter that I am the second prince in line to the throne—beings still attempt to torment me. It's safer in pairs, particularly when it was the two of us princes. Together our powers made us dangerous enough to discourage any bold beings. We used to spend every waking moment together; now I do everything on my own. There are no other younglings my age in the palace.

Well, I guess that is not entirely true. Balric is only a couple of years younger than us, but he has barely a drop of power. He constantly whines about it and tries to blame us for his shortcomings. I would rather be alone than put up with his company any night. My ears would start bleeding after only a few hours in his presence, listening to his whining.

The only time Ciaran acknowledges me is when we are tormenting Balric. I am not sure if it's because *he* wants to, or if it has something to do with how much his father enjoys watching us plague the gnat. It could be a little of both.

Whatever the reason is behind Ciaran's sudden abandonment, it's starting to really piss me off. Does he think he's too good for me all of a sudden? What an arrogant prick!

I port back to the chambers I share with my parents. I have been spending more and more time with them lately, since I have nothing else to do. Unlike Ciaran's, my parents are as affectionate as any member of the Night Court could let themselves be.

They always listened to the stories I would come back with from adventures, and took an active role in my training. It had been *my* father who taught us to port, not the stupid king. It was *my* mother who taught us how to tie our treasures to us. My parents have always been better parents to Ciaran than his own. His sudden absence seems to weigh heavy on them, and that adds to my anger.

"Kes?" I hear my mother call from inside the study.

"Yes, Mother?" I ask with a tone that has me flinching. My mother tolerates a lot, but giving her attitude was not one of them.

"Kestrel, Prince of the Night Court, get your feathered ass in here!" she barks. Great, she used my full name. I *hate* my full name. I swear she uses it only because she knows I despise it.

Kestrel…what a stupid name.

I make every sound of complaint I can think of as I stomp my way down the hall towards the study. She's already mad, I might as well really go for it. The night is already bad; why not make it worse?

"Yes, *Mother*?" I really lay into the attitude this time. She snaps her red eyes towards me, staring at me down her beak. I got all my bird-like features from her and my coloring from my father. Her feathers are emerald green, and if the feathers of my hair are to be believed, I will have pitch black ones. I have to wait to find out, several more years, until I hit puberty.

Whatever that is.

For now, I am covered in these short, fluffy, gray downy feathers. They are the bane of my existence. Why could I not have gotten my father's wings? The same wings Ciaran and his father have? At least then I would only have to deal with the awkward growth of my wings. Not only do the feathers give other beings plenty of ammunition for torment, but they are also such a pain to take care of. I hate them. At least I do not have a beak.

"Kestrel! What is the meaning of such bold behavior?" She has this way of looking at me that always makes me fold. I feel my entire body sag in defeat as I groan; it came out as a whine even to my own ears. The anger I have been feeding for months at Ciaran suddenly feels like a wound instead as I drag myself over to my mother and climb up into her lap.

It's something we have been doing for as long as I can remember—a necessity when you have feathers, and *not* because I need comforting. I sit in my mother's lap, and she uses her beak to preen the feathers on my head while her hands work on my wings. The familiar motions instantly calm me. We sit in silence for the time it takes her to finish.

"Now, tell me what it is that bothers you so, my son," she says, removing one last useless feather from my wings. It's easier to speak to her about the weird feelings inside me while facing away from her like this. I do not like talking about them.

"Ciaran...he has been acting stra—"

Father chooses that exact moment to port into the study. I was about to groan when I notice my father frantically running over to where we sit. My father never does anything quickly. He crouches down so he's eye level with my mother, and the two of them share a look I have never been able to decipher.

"Listen, both of you," he says, clasping one of each of our hands with his own. I feel a weird fluttering in my stomach, and I feel the burn of tears behind my eyes. "My brother has just declared me a traitor." My mother gasps, while I try to figure out what that means.

"No, whatever for?" My mother says in clear disbelief, with a decent amount of terror.

"That is not impo—"

"What does that mean?" I ask, feeling like I am several steps behind my parents, who share another one of those looks. It always feels like they are having a conversation with their eyes.

"It means that I will be gone soon," my father replies. If he's simply going somewhere, why is he so frantic?

"For how long?" I ask, thinking it must be a very long time if he's this upset about it.

"Forever, my son. This is the last time I will be able to speak to you." I cannot believe his words. Surely mother and I can go with him, or at least visit.

"Can we not come with you or visit?" Everything about this conversation was making me dizzy and the fluttering in my stomach only grew.

"No, son...I am to be executed." There it is, the fluttering sensation and the burning tears clicking into place—dread. Somehow my body knew before my brain that something terrible was going to happen.

"Now, listen to me. Neither of you are to intervene. I do not want his eyes to land on either of you and take this madness any further. Do you both hear me?" Whenever my father speaks, it always sounds like there is a joke hidden within his words; he did not sound that way now. I feel something wet on my face, but cannot focus on anything but my father and the whooshing sound in my ears.

"Are you certain?" My mother's voice sounds far away.

"Very. He claims to hear *whispers* that lead him to find long lost items and tell him secrets he would have no way of knowing without them. I had a few choice words for him, not only for his crazy claims, but for what he's doing to his son." My mother gasps again.

"Why would you risk doing such a thing?" My mother's voice shook with both rage and something else. It sounds like fear, and if my mother is afraid, then I need to be as well.

"Someone *had* to try to reason with him, but unfortunately, he's far past reason." He sounds sad, like he's mourning my uncle instead of his own death.

"What is he doing to Ciaran?" Maybe whatever he's doing has something to do with my cousin's strange behavior.

"Never you mind that, Kes. Do you hear me?" I can only nod. "Do not judge your cousin's actions too harshly...he's only trying to survive. That is all you need to know. Promise me, Kestrel. Promise you will not dig further and that you will not hold your cousin's actions against him." This time when I hear my full name I cherish it, afraid it will be the last time I ever hear it come from my father's lips.

"I promise." I barely get the words out before a spelled scroll appears requesting our prompt presence in the throne room.

"Eternity would not be enough time to tell you both everything I wish I could right now." He kisses the top of my head in a rare show of affection before turning to my mother. "You will have to keep out of sight as best you can, and I fear for what your life will look like more than I fear losing my own. Teach him everything you can. He's already too much like me," he says to my mother with a wink, sounding like himself once again.

"It's time. Port to the back of the room and stay hidden." They do that thing with their eyes again before he adds, "Try not to watch." My mother can only nod before my father ports away, and not even a moment later my mother ports us to the back of the throne room.

I watch as my father approaches the throne with his head held high, and I can see my uncle's mouth moving, but I can not hear anything over the deafening sound inside my head. Everything is moving so quickly and yet it feels like time has stopped all at once. I am vaguely aware of the beings around us cheering at whatever it is my uncle has just declared.

Two things happen next that I do not think I will ever be able to forget for as long as I live. First, my father kneels as Ciaran comes to stand next to him, his body moving in unnaturally jerky movements. He holds a long obsidian sword in his hand. My father says something to Ciaran with open kindness written all over his face. A slight nod is all Ciaran seems capable of giving before my father leans over the wooden block in front of him.

Second, my mother covers my eyes just as my head decides to silence the pounding that has been keeping me deaf prior. It's just in time to hear the sound of a sword swinging through the air, followed by the sound of it coming into contact with flesh. I hear this sound twice before the sound of something heavy and wet hitting the ground. Cheers rise up around me.

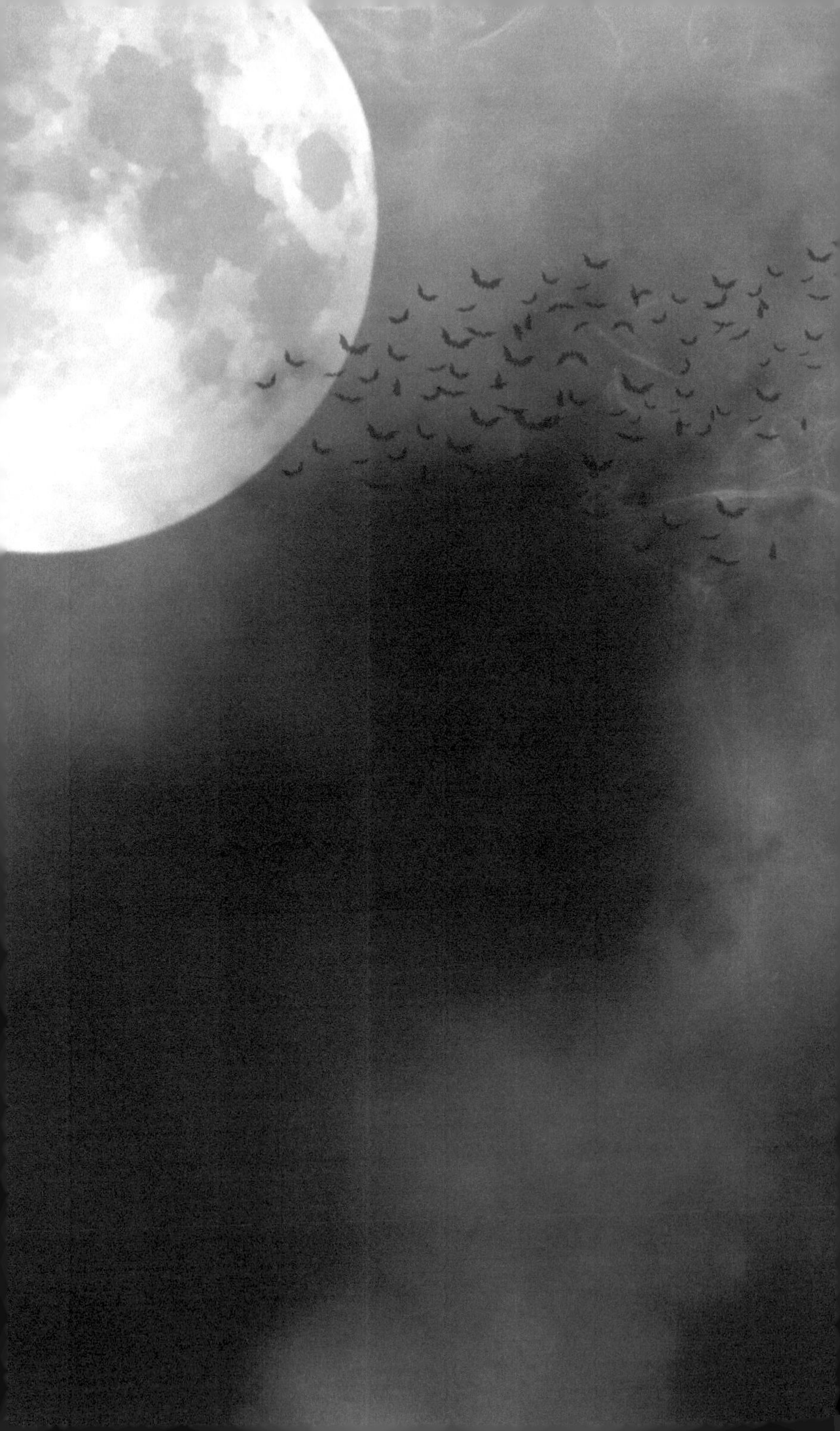

THREE

CIARAN

16 Years Old

Kes and his mother enter the throne room, causing the entire space to come to an abrupt hush. They always have that effect anywhere they go, ever since his father was absurdly convicted of treason. He had been the first and the last being to speak on my behalf. I will never forget the look of horror that took over his face when my father proudly showed him what his new toy would allow him to do to me. He said something about that type of magic being forbidden in the realm for a reason.

Shortly after those words left my uncle's lips, my father sentenced him to death for treason. I was frozen in the ridiculous position my father had left me in when he was showing off his control over me, forgotten for the mo-ment. No one could see or hear the horror I felt at the conviction, but it was nothing compared to the horror I felt during the execution.

My uncle had been one of the only beings in my life to show me kindness. He took the time to teach me ways to use my power when my own father had been too busy doing who knows what, but most likely on one of his wild hunts *the whispers* he was always speaking of took him on.

My father is crazy. Not in the figurative sense; he's legitimately insane. He said something about *the whispers* to my uncle before having me contort myself into whatever abstract position he chose. But after my uncle's reaction, he never spoke of them to anyone besides myself and my mother.

I do not think my mother actually hears anything around her. She wears the same expression and holds the same glass always filled with wine, while her eyes stare through something only she can see. The only thing that ever changes is the clothing she wears. I often wonder if my father has not placed a spelled object upon her as well. If he has, it must be hidden, because none of the jewelry she wears has the same dark red coloring to the metal, plus it changes nearly every night.

If the court knew my father was listening to what the voices in his head were telling him to do, I think they would find a way to get rid of him. As much as the idea pleases me, it cannot happen. Not if I want to become the king some night.

Since my father had seen to the execution of the only other grown male in line for the throne, it will fall to me or Kes. Neither of us are strong enough to take the throne and keep it. Not yet, at least.

Every time I see my cousin I am reminded of the day his father was killed, by my own hands. The first strike with the sword had not been enough to fully sever his head. The way his body jerked as blood spilled from him until the second strike ended his torment is forever burned into my memory. I think my father did it on purpose. He had been the one in control of my body, and I could never be certain if it was my own weakness or my father's wickedness that had been the cause of my uncle's unnecessary torment.

It has become easy to see through my cousin, as if he were invisible. Distancing myself several years ago was something I had to actively work at, but now, I do not even have to think about it. At first it was something I felt I had to do to keep him safe before morphing into shame every time I caught a glimpse of him. Now, I do not think I care enough to concern myself with his safety or shame, for that matter.

Where I once grieved the loss of my companion, I now long for the moments I have to myself. They are few and far between thanks to my father. I am his personal puppet; when he pulls strings, I do as he wishes. I hated my father before he placed this curse on my finger, but I still craved his approval like the naive youngling I once was. He can take his approval and shove it up his ass, because the only thing I crave from him anymore is his death. Preferably a slow and torturous one.

At least once every week, my father drains my well of power entirely causing me to succumb to the forced sleep an empty well demands. The feel of him pulling my power from me used to bother me. It's an unsettling feeling, but I grew accustomed to it quickly.

I used to speak up if he was getting close to the bottom of my well, and he would stop siphoning it away long enough for it to refill. I soon realized if I said nothing he would not have access to me for at least a couple of nights. The older I get the faster my well seems to recover. Luckily he has not caught on, and I have been able to steal a night here and there to myself.

Every moment I have I am in one of the libraries in the palace looking for any information on this damned ring or the metal it's made from. I have not been able to find anything, not even a single line of text about objects used to control other beings.

If I could go back in time I would...do what?

Likely nothing. I might be getting older, but I am still nothing more than a whelp. Something my father enjoys reminding me of. My claws have not changed much from that night several years ago when I tried to remove my hand. My wings are still small and can barely pick me up off the ground. I have grown taller, though it has only made my body feel foreign and clumsy. No matter who is in control of me, I never feel as though my body is my own.

My father has kept me standing here next to him like a sentinel for hours. It seems unfair that I should have no control over my body but still have to feel the pain it endures. I dare not voice my opinion for it would only make my situation worse. I learned that the hard way—not that I could speak if I wanted to right now anyway.

I watch as my cousin and his mother approach the throne. Kes walks with a limp he's trying to mask, and there is a fresh bruise under his left eye. Someone or *someones* must have intercepted him moments before he arrived.

I do not care.

"My king, you requested our presence?" my aunt asks softly. It's strange to see her hide away the strong female she had once been. She used to be impossible to miss in a crowd with her once vibrant feathers. Now she seems muted, both in appearance and in demeanor.

"Ah, my traitorous brother's little feathered family." The room laughs perfectly on cue. "We seem to have more traitors to deal with." My aunt is unnaturally still while Kes is practically vibrating with anger. Both manage to keep their eyes downcast and say nothing. "I thought perhaps you would enjoy witnessing their executions, for memory's sake."

"Of course," my aunt responds after a long moment of silence.

"Wonderful, now go away and find some place to stand. All the feathers disgust me." The room laughs again as the two walk off to hide in a corner. My father claps his hands together a few times and within moments I move to drag two random high fae out of the audience; their expressions a mix of confusion and dread.

They are not traitors. My father has a habit of creating false traitors for the excuse to put on an execution. More than anything, I think he enjoys controlling me in a room filled with beings and no one except the two of us know-ing, since mother never leaves the chambers.

I drag the first one in front of the same wooden block Kes's father had leaned over years ago. The fae drops to his knees. He has to know there is no way out of this situation as I push his head down towards the block. The last thing he says just as my sword finds its mark is a confused "why" before his head is severed with one strike.

I stopped feeling anything for the fae of the Night Court after I severed dozens of heads for my father's farce of an execution. In the beginning it felt wrong to kill my own when they had committed no crime, but now I find I rather enjoy it.

The second fae seems to be in a daze as he stumbles toward the block still dripping with the blood from the male before him. I kick the headless fae's body to the side making room for this one to kneel, but he does not.

"My mate…," he says so softly that I doubt anyone be-sides my father and I hear it.

"NO!" a female shouts as she shoves her way through the crowd. No one moves easily for her. "He has done nothing! He's no traitor, I would *know*!" The female is getting closer to the front of the crowd, and based on the look my father wears, there will be three executions today.

"Katalia, stop! Are you trying to get yourself killed?" the fae says. His voice is full of fear, and it takes me a moment to realize it's not for himself but for the female still shoving her way through unmoving bodies. "My king, she does not know what she's saying..."

"I know exactly what I am saying—he's my true mate! There would be no keeping any treasonous activity from me." Her next words seal her fate. "You must be mistaken!" The sharp inhales from the crowd say they know her end is near as well.

"Katalia, please...," the male pleads with the doomed female.

"What does it matter? If you are dead I will not be long behind you. The mate bond will demand it," she seethes. Whatever this mate bond is sounds like a horrible curse. The idea of having my survival dependent upon another's is something I would never want.

"But the...," the male is unable to finish his sentence as the female finally pushes her way out of the crowd. Her stomach is oddly rounded. I am slow to comprehend that she carries a youngling in her stomach, which is why it protrudes in such an odd way. I had only seen a pregnant female a couple of times before now.

I am so distracted, I do not notice the male has found his way to his knees until I am pushing his head down onto the block. My father has yet to say anything about the outburst from the female. I lift my sword and swing it down with enough force so the head is severed with one stroke.

The noise the female releases the moment the male dies is startling. She clutches at her chest as if she's physically in pain and tears stream freely down her cheeks. Something about the way she responded makes me uncomfortable. I have never seen anyone this open with their emotions. Whatever she's experiencing seems far worse than grief.

"You *monster*!" she screams at my father. He still says nothing, but I feel my feet start to move in her direction. Something in my stomach begins to flutter as I wrap my hand around her arm.

"And *you*!" This time her venom is directed at me as I drag her toward the block. "This young and already such a horrid creature. You will be much worse than your father. No wonder your mother ran away inside her own mind so many years ago. I would not be able to stand it knowing I birthed a creature as foul as you!"

This is not the first time a fae to be executed has unleashed their rage upon me with words, but this is the first time it made me flinch internally.

Could I be the reason my mother is the way she is?

I replay her words over and over in my head, searching for the truth within them. I am fully caught up in my own mind that I do not even realize my sword is raised until it swings down upon her neck. Her head lays next to her mate's. Their noses touch as if even in death they are still drawn to the other.

I do not like the way it makes me feel.

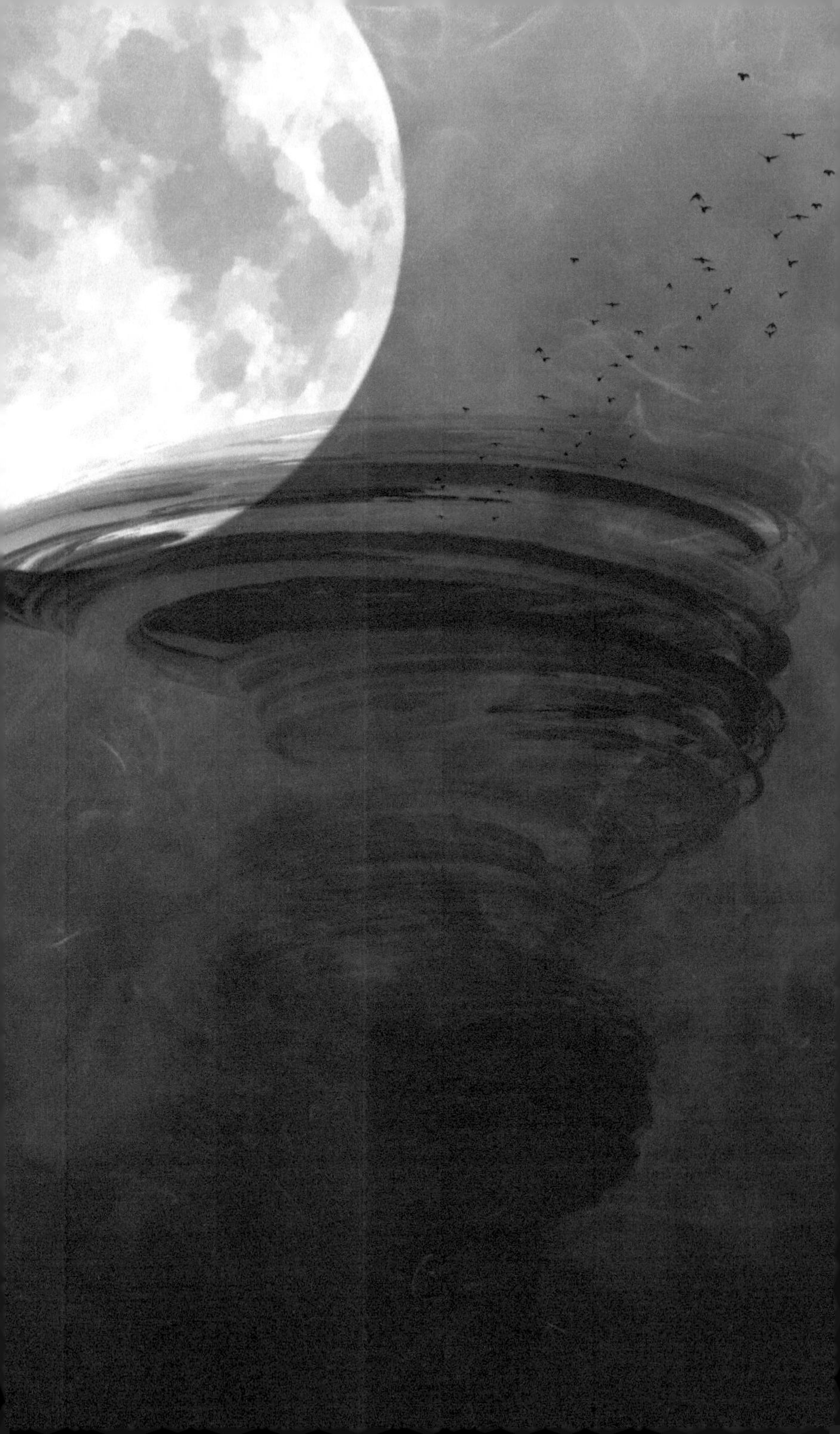

Four

KES

20 Years Old

The harsh laughter of the being standing over me sounds like they have a throat full of glass. I have no idea who they are, but it's not uncommon for me to meet someone new from this position. When the whole court enjoys tormenting you, it makes it rare to face the same fae twice. A shove from behind me had sent me sprawling face first onto the floor of the library. Luckily, my reflexes have been getting faster, and I was able to catch myself before my face smashed into the ground...again.

"Traitor spawn," the being says as if it's the most original insult they can imagine. How dull their mind must be.

"Wow. *So* original. I just might cry," I say, giving my best fake sad face. The encounters used to feel like little cuts to my soul each time they happened. Now, they are just obnoxious. I stand up and dust myself off before adopting a casual stance and letting a grin cut across my face.

A little over a year ago, I noticed that acting as if I was unaffected and instead looking at them like they were the ones being laughed at made them uncomfortable. Since then, I have been working on perfecting it. I like the look their faces make when they realize I robbed them of the reaction they were hoping for.

"Honestly, that was the best you could come up with? Do you know how many equally daft fae have used those exact words? My gods, a youngling half my age could have come up with something far more creative." There it is, the crease of confusion between the brows. Next will come the anger, and I will either be sporting a new injury for the next few hours, or I will be able to walk away while they stand there in shock. Either way, I always feel like I win.

"You should try reading to expand your vocabulary." I gesture to the multitude of books around us. "Maybe then you could come up with something more original. 'Quisling warbler' or maybe 'recreant progeny' would have been my choice. Personally, I am a fan of the bird insults. They feel more curated and they amuse me. Honestly, if that was the best you could do, I would hate to see how minuscule your brain is. I can not imagine being of lesser intelligence than a youngling at your age. Tell me, what does that feel like?" I ask with a smile he cannot misconstrue as anything but mocking.

"You...you..." The spluttering is a good sign I will be walking away unscathed. I cannot wait till the night I am grown enough to instill fear into the beings who dare to touch me.

"Yes, me." I wave my hands in a gesture indicating he should hurry and choose his words already. "I know we live for a long time, however, sometime this year would be great." The fae has yellowish orange skin that is now almost fluorescent with rage. It looks like maybe I am *not* going to walk away unscathed after all.

"Oh, look at you glowing like a Day fae." If I am going to get hit I may as well make it count.

"You little fluff—"

"Oh yes, please insult my fluffy gray youngling feathers. I am so offended." I place my hands on either side of my face and pretend to be horrified.

Definitely not walking away from this one.

"Just remember, I still have many years of growth ahead of me. You do not, and I do not forget faces." The fae is squaring off in preparation to strike, pausing at my words long enough for me to say, "exactly," before turning on my taloned feet and walking away. I tense preparing for a hit or another shove—neither come.

My father taught me, in the few short years I had with him, some basic fighting skills. I have been reading as many books as I can to teach myself some more advanced techniques, and my mother has been teaching me to use my power and my magic. We share the same air element. Someday I will be able to take the air from someone's lungs before they even have a chance to touch me.

My body is still too awkward to be any kind of respectable when it comes to fighting. Everything I have read makes it sound like a form of dance that requires grace. My wings are uneven, which often throws off my balance, and the fluffy gray feathers are starting to be replaced with long black feathers that, when caught in the right light, have a faint purple hue.

My wings will be magnificent, and I think I will be quite the terrifying sight when I am grown. I wish I would hurry up and get there because the itch of my shedding feathers is bound to drive me mad. If it were not for my mother helping preen me, I would be lost to madness already.

As soon as I am out of the fae's sight, I port back to the chambers I share with my mother. I notice the study's door cracked open which means my mother is in there. She warded the chambers as soon as I learned to port, making it so I could only port into the parlor, having to walk by the study and their room to get to mine.

"Kes," my mother calls out. I had not made a noise and yet she always seems to know when I am here. My mother is the only being in this realm I care anything for. I am pretty sure I love her and she loves me, yet I am also not sure what love looks like, making me uncertain.

Normally, I do not mind spending time with my mother, but right now I want to get to my room to practice the techniques I read about earlier while they are fresh in my mind. Maybe I can listen to whatever she has to say and then quickly retreat. I will just keep repeating in my mind everything I need to remember.

When I push open the door, one look at my mother and I know something is off. Her feathers are fluffed out the way they get when she's flustered. And, she's pacing. My mother does not pace. She's calm, logical, and always has a plan.

"What's wrong, Mother?" I want to take the question back the second her eyes connect with my own. It has been years since I have seen her this distraught, and that night had not ended well for either of us. A fluttering begins in my stomach.

"The king has requested our presence in the throne room this second night." Which is never a good request to receive, yet it was not necessarily bad either. It means we will be forced to witness more senseless Night fae deaths.

Death does not bother me, nor does torture for that matter; they both intrigue me. It's something about the range of colors we hold within our blood and the sounds different places on the body can elicit with the right technique. The only thing that does bother me is how wrong it feels to kill our own. Everyone knows none of the fae convicted are actually traitors, although their own logic does not seem to apply to my father, in their minds.

"What do you think he wants? You are not usually this upset over a summons." I cannot see what the big deal is; however, something inside me is setting off warnings.

"Have you forgotten what happened ten years ago tonight?" she asks me.

"That was ten years ago? Tonight?" That explains the fluttering.

"Yes, and there is no way your uncle has forgotten what tonight is either." She locks her red eyes with my own, the same red as hers, and holds my gaze for a moment. I try to swallow the thing stuck in my throat a few times. It will not go away.

"Kes, you must do *whatever* I say when we are in front of your uncle. Do you understand?" While I do understand, I do not like the look in my mother's eyes.

"Mother, I cannot do *nothing* if there is something I *can* do. Besides, for all we know nothing will come of your worries." I know the words are a lie the second they leave my lips, and it's clear my mother knows as well.

"You will do exactly as I say. You will let me do my role as your mother. Do you *hear* me, Kestrel?" My heart begins to beat faster, and I cannot make my mouth form any words. The last time I spoke with my father, he used my full name. I cannot control the dread that begins building into a heavy weight inside me.

What if this is the last time I speak to my mother?

"Mother, can I ask you something? It's a bit strange, I think." I did not say the things I wish I had to my father before he died, and I am not taking any chances with my mother, even if it's embarrassing.

"Of course," she says, sounding a little thrown off by my sudden change of topic.

"What does love feel like?" Her face softens and she takes my hand in hers.

"Love is when you are willing to place another above your own needs. Love is when the thought of losing that being causes the breath to leave your lungs. You not only want them in your life—you *need* them. To lose them would be to become a shell of the being you once were. Love is horrible, and yet it's the most wonderful feeling in the entire realm." Her answer confuses me. I have felt some of these things, but not all of them. She must see the uncertainty in my eyes.

"There are different kinds of love. I loved your father in the way Night fae are capable of, though we were not true mates. However, there is only one being in all the realms who I love so fully there is not a single thing I would not do for them." The back of my eyes feel hot for some reason.

"Who?" My voice comes out in a near whisper.

"You, my son. I would turn the moon into the sun to spare you any hurt. I would stand before you in the face of any foe. This is my duty as your mother, and I do it happily. There is no greater joy I have ever had than the day you were brought into this realm. No matter what the future holds for us, I want you to remember something. You have not only been loved, but you are worthy of love, and no matter where or what I am in the realm, I will always love you."

I am stunned. I have never heard words like this spoken—ever. If my parents said such things to each other, it had never been in front of me. The way my mother easily lets them flow from her mouth makes me feel something. I am not sure what it is, though I think perhaps it must be love.

"I love you, too, Mother." I manage to squeak out, and for the first time in my life, *I* reach out to hug my mother. We hold on to each other for a moment before my mother pulls away. She holds me by the shoulders and looks at me for a long moment, as if taking stock of all the changes that have been occurring in me.

"You have already grown so much, and I can see the male you will someday be in the shadows of your face. You got the best parts of both of us, you know? You got your mother's good looks," she said with a smirk. "And your father's humor. Do not let that die in this place." It feels like she's saying goodbye.

"Well now, shall we go see what this mad king wants?" I want to say no. So badly do I want to say no, but I know that is not the answer my mother needs from me.

A few moments later we stood in front of my uncle and cousin. Ciaran's presence is not a surprise, and over the years I have noticed things I had not when he first began ignoring me—the way only his eyes seemed to speak, and they were always in conflict with his actions. He never moves with any kind of grace, and while we are both awkward with youth, his jerky movements appear to pain him. I have no idea what happened to my cousin, but my father's words stuck with me.

Do not judge your cousin's actions too harshly, he's only trying to survive.

I must have gotten lost in my own mind for a few minutes because I am surprised when my mother steps forward and boldly tells my uncle, "No."

No, what?

"We never would have told him of any of our plans. He's only a youngling, why would we trust him to keep a secret?"

What is she talking about?

"You finally admit to committing treason with my brother?"

What?

"If it's as you say, we would never involve our son." The king narrows his eyes at her. She had not actually admitted to anything, which has not been lost on him.

"Perhaps you need a little time to think about your answer." He snaps his fingers and a hook lowers from the tall ceiling. It descends at such a slow speed, I am certain it's on purpose to build fear, and it's working.

"Mother?" She snaps her eyes to me. There is no regret or hesitation in them.

"Hush, you will do as you are told. Do not forget I am your mother." It comes out in a harsh disciplinary way, but I know what she really means. I give her a slight nod in acceptance while her eyes take me in one last time, like she's trying to burn me into her memory.

"You will go and stand in the same corner you watched your father's demise from. What a great way to commemorate his anniversary." There is a moment where I nearly open my mouth, ready with one of my smart ass remarks, until I see the determination in my mother's eyes. I know she's already sacrificing herself for the sake of me, and I will not make it worse for her.

I watch as my mother stands to her full height and holds her head high for the first time since my father's death. She had been making herself small and unobtrusive for the last ten years in an attempt to not draw any unwanted attention to us. The same female who meticulously preened my feathers and, not long ago, declared her love for me makes a terrifying sight. She looks magnificent.

I port to the corner of the room and can no longer hear the words spoken between them clearly. The hook finally lowers to its final position. My uncle gets up and lifts my mother as if she weighs nothing. Piercing her wings and skin, he digs the hook into the flesh of her back and hangs her upon it.

She tries to not scream. I can see her trying, but the hook is a rare metal that causes an adverse reaction to fae. I think it's called "iron." I try to remember everything I have ever read about iron in an attempt to escape the scene in front of me.

My uncle sits back on his throne as Ciaran walks forward in his stilted way. I can see him take several deep breaths, even from where I hide in the corner with the shadows. My mother's screams start to fade as she regains control over her pain. She says something to my cousin, I doubt anyone but the two of them can hear, before he picks up a hooked knife and begins to slice into her.

Death and torture may not bother me, but when it's my mother it does. Watching my cousin cut ribbons of flesh from her makes my father's words harder to recall. I struggle to escape into my mind again, yet it's impossible to look away as the one being I have left in this realm is reduced to pieces.

When I think the torture is over and I am finally able to take my mother back to our chambers where I can help her heal, my uncle stands from his throne once again and speaks to my barely-conscious mother. Whatever she says in return, he does not like. He unhooks her and drops her to the floor, causing her to land hard on her knees. With a snap of his fingers, the same wooden block my father died upon appears in front of her.

With her last bit of strength, she somehow finds me in the shadows and says loud enough for me to hear, "Do not forget." She continues to stare at me, even as Ciaran pushes her down onto the block.

"I will not," I say quietly, but my mother must have read the words on my lips. She gives a slight nod, closes her eyes, and lets out one last breath as the sword comes down across her neck, taking not only her head, but a bit of the top of one wing with it.

Three swings of his sword is all it takes for everything I have to be ripped away. I have only cared for three beings in this entire realm, and one of the three has stolen the other two from me. He just took the only being I had left—the only being I have ever loved.

I feel the breath leave my lungs and something wither away inside me. If this is love, I never want to feel it again. Love feels like dying, and I will *never* let myself love another again.

I banish my father's words from my mind. I *will* judge Ciaran, and I will judge him harshly. I will never forgive him for this. He could be a puppet on a string for all I care; he will always wear my parents' deaths on his face.

For some reason the image of Ciaran on strings with half of his face as my father's severed head and the other half as my mother's made me start to laugh. My laughter is chaotic and grows more and more out of control until I am bent over at the waist with my hands on my knees laughing a maniac's laugh.

I finally get control of myself. I stand as tall as I can and hold my head high. The entire room is quiet and they all look at me, most with horrified expressions. I lock eyes with my cousin for the first time in over a decade, and I stare at him.

I let him see exactly what I think of him. No longer will I search for an excuse for his actions. I will judge them as harshly as he deserves. I mouth three words to him, not wasting the one time he has acknowledged my existence over the last several years.

"I hate you."

Five
CIARAN

20 Years Old

There was no mistaking the words my cousin intended for me and me alone. I had not allowed myself to truly see him in so long that it came as a shock to see the metamorphosis he was undergoing. I am also aware of my own physical changes, though I never thought much about them. I never thought much about anything beyond ridding myself of this fucking ring.

He hates me and I do not blame him, nor do I care. I have grown immune to torture and death over the years. I learned to love it—crave it even—however, I do not love being covered in my aunt's blood. She tried to absolve me of my crimes against her before I even committed them, but I did not accept her forgiveness.

I truly am wicked. While I do not relish that it's my aunt's blood coating me, I do savor the blood. I did not want to torture my aunt, and yet, I enjoyed it. I did not want to kill her, but I felt *nothing* when I removed her head. No remorse, but also none of the wicked delight I have become accustomed to.

I knew what my father was going to have me do the second they arrived, and I mentally raged against it. I did not wish for my aunt's demise, however, in the end I did take pleasure in it. I really am my father's son, and I despise myself for being anything like him.

I have been watching him over the past several years as he fell deeper into his insanity. He speaks out loud to the voices in his head, and a couple years ago, I began to worry it might be something passed down through the generations. I refuse to become the creature my father has. When I become the monster I will inevitably be, it will be of my own making.

The illness taking over my father's mind is the one in control of him. I listen to his one-sided conversations with whatever it is he thinks he's speaking to. It will lead him in an entirely different direction and have him believing it was his own idea—which I suppose it is. Even though it's his own mind, he's still controlled by the illness that rots it. I have had enough of being controlled by another to last me a lifetime.

While searching for a way to remove this shackle from my finger, I stumbled across several journals of past kings. The oldest journal rarely mentioned any kind of *whispers* or voices in their head. However, starting with my great grandfather, then my grandfather, and now my father, they all speak of *whispers* and a witch's curse—three generations in a row. I wonder when the illness will begin to plague me.

The thought of being controlled my entire life until my father's death, only to then be controlled by some rotting illness of the mind, sounds like an existence not worth having. Perhaps if I return my being to the realm and come back in a later life my situation would be better. All I need is full autonomy and from there what becomes of my existence is in my hands alone, which is all I really want—to live my life the way I see fit.

I barely remember the first half of my life. It was the only time I had ever been free, and all I can remember are a few moments in the woods making discoveries with my cousin. The cousin who now hates me for taking from him the one good thing he had—parents.

I do not care.

I was always shocked when we returned from our adventures and his parents listened to every inconsequential bit of information we thought to be profound. And they did not just listen, they asked us questions and shared in our excitement. I always wished my parents were more like his.

My mother, as far as I can remember, has always been a walking corpse. Her facial expression never changes, she never seems aware of her surroundings, and she's always drinking wine from the same cup—night in and night out. Over the last several years, my suspicions have grown into a probability that my father has something to do with her current state.

When I executed the fated pair a few years ago, I began looking into what happened to my mother. By all accounts, she lost herself to her mind a couple of years after I was born. If it were not for the way my father controls her, I would think that female may have been correct when she said I was the reason my mother was a shell of her former self. If my father was able to find a way to control me, it's entirely possible he found a way to control her as well.

The only time she shows any reaction is when my father tells her to. He will make a statement, then grab her arm and say something like, "Do you agree?" and she will simply nod her head. If I cared anything for her, I would attempt to free her from his grasp as well, but I do not.

My father's desire for ultimate control and power has made him as much a slave to himself as he has made me a slave to him. He's no longer in control of his own life, driven by his hunger for a different form of sustenance. I know he's taking something from each fae I execute through his will. I am not sure what or how he does it, but I notice the following day he's *different*. The mania he gets when he has depleted my well and is close to doing the same to his own makes him hostile and takes away any sanity he has left until he absorbs his next source of power.

Several nights ago, he had me execute nine fae in quick succession, the most he ever sentenced to death at one time. After, he ported us to his study and was calm, in the way beings get after consuming too much wine. His words were slower and bled into each other as he walked around the room that had once contained a multitude of books. It now holds nothing but bottles, burners, and elaborate twisting glass canisters that are always dripping pungent liquids onto a piece of strange metal or gem. He called them "experiments" and claimed "the whispers" told him how to do each one.

He told me about a curse placed on our line a few generations past; I imagine it's the one I read about in those journals. I listened as he lamented repeatedly over the reduction of our power. An injustice placed upon us by a witch who stole half our power from us. Eventually he was no longer speaking to me directly, and I listened to him have another one-sided conversation.

Not once during his entire rant did he mention a way to break the curse. There is always a way, the land demands a balance. Young as I am, even I know that much. He prioritizes his search for more power over the solution to the curse itself, making it clear he does not wish to end the curse a fraction as much as he wishes to continue to absorb new sources. Fulfilling his desires has only increased his need for more and more power. I do not think he could go even one full night without siphoning away my power or absorbing it from another. His need comes before all else, and the *whispers* encourage it.

Not being able to access my own power has really become the worst part of this enslavement. Some second nights, like this one, when my father has become drunk off power, he locks me in my room. If I had my power I could easily escape and port to search the libraries and archives.

I check all of the doors and windows to see if any open. My father is bound to forget one at some point, and when he left a few moments ago he was particularly sloppy. He stumbled through the room, wildly throwing his power—my power—around. Even his words came out slurred. Kes's mother must have contained a deep well of power for him to be in such a state.

Click.

For a moment, I stare at the open window. I have checked these windows so many times over the last several years, and while I always wished for one to open, I never truly expected it to happen. The breeze blows in through the opening and brings with it the scent of freedom. I immediately begin to climb out into the fresh air, not willing to waste any time in case my father decides he's not done with me for the night.

I take a moment to breathe in the crisp night air when it occurs to me—I have not been outside since my father took me into the woods however many years ago. The moonlight on my skin and the fresh air in my lungs invigorate me. My freedom waits, and all I need to do is climb down this tower and make my way to the ground below—far below.

There is not much for me to grip onto and my wings are useless for flying; the uneven growth of each wing makes balancing difficult. Each inch down is a struggle, and I have several stories to descend before I have to make my way around the tower to reach the roof of the palace below. I feel an urgency that makes me pick up the pace and I begin choosing my hand holds and footing faster.

My right foot slips out from under me while I move my left into position. For a brief second, I dangle a few feet below the window I exited at the top of the tower, with nothing between me and the ground below. If my claws were fully grown, I would have been able to hold on, and if my wings were less awkward, I could at least glide through the air.

Wind whips through my hair as I silently plummet to the ground. I open my worthless wings on instinct, but all that succeeds in doing is sending me into a tailspin. This is not the freedom I wished for, but it's still freedom. I tuck my wings back in and open my arms to embrace the end of my father's control. Before I collide with the terrain below, a smirk cuts across my face as I think of my father's reaction when he first realizes he no longer has my power to claim as his own—only, the collision does not happen.

I jerk to a stop with my nose an inch from the ground for only a breath before my body collapses into the dirt of the garden I land in. Confusion clouds my mind as I pick myself up and quickly make my way down to the edge of the woods. In the distance, the peaks of The Nocturia Mountains are visible. I have been thinking, if I am unable to remove the ring, then perhaps I can get far enough away to end the hold my father has on me.

The ring!

It should have occurred to me that the ring would never let me die. If I had taken two seconds to think about it, I would have jumped directly out the window. I am mildly disappointed, death would have been a guaranteed way to remove my father's grip on my power. It's only a guess that distance will do the trick.

I run in the beginning, trying to gain as much distance as quickly as possible. By the next night my pace dramatically slows. Not having access to my power means my body recovers at a normal pace. I may as well be a lesser fae.

I need to check my location and make sure I am still going in the direction of the Nocturia Mountains. I do not think my father will look for me there, and I bet I can find a decent cave to hold out in. What I will do after that, I am not sure. I am really hoping the ring will come off on its own once I am far enough away.

A tall tree with low boughs is coming up ahead of me. I can climb it all the way up to get a look at my surroundings. It will make me far more visible if my father happens to be flying overhead looking for me; however, since I have yet to feel the pull of my power, he's either still riding the wave from my aunt's power, or I am right about distance. It's still too soon to know for sure, but I am certain I will feel the pull of power before my father even lays eyes on me.

It has been a long time since I climbed a tree, and I remember it being difficult without the use of power. Kes and I would have races to see who could reach the top faster. We decided the use of power was cheating. I am taller and stronger than I was then, making it much easier to reach the branches above and quickly climb to the top.

It's a good thing I came up to check my trajectory, because I was starting to go south of the mountains. Luckily I am not too far off, not that it really matters since my only goal is to get as far away as possible. I do not bother climbing back down and instead jump, getting whipped by a few errant branches on the way, and come to the same abrupt stop just above the ground before landing softly on my feet.

It's concerning to me how the ring still blocks my power, yet I am still unable to remove it. Maybe I have not gotten as far enough away as I thought. I correct my direction and pick up as much speed as I can while filled with the paranoia that I will feel the pull any moment.

Hours go by and I still have yet to feel my father's control. I climb another tree to check my direction once more and notice the crescent moon now hung in the sky. There is no way my father will go a full night without siphoning power away from me. This has to be far enough away, and yet, I still cannot not remove the damned ring.

There has to be someone with the knowledge I seek, someone who can remove the unassuming band that has been expanding perfectly with my finger as I grow. I wish I could find a way, then I will not fear my father locating me. I hate the way fear makes my stomach flip and a sweat break out that has nothing to do with my physical exhaustion.

I need to rest, but fear doing so because my father could fly the distance I have put between us in mere moments. I cannot rest until I am in the mountains, and even once I reach them, I am uncertain it will be enough to keep me out of his clutches for good. Somehow, I still need to be able to continue looking for answers, if only they would simply appear.

About an hour later I find myself standing at the entrance of a clearing in the woods. In the center is a strange little mushroom hut that looks like it has seen better nights. There is so much power in the area I can almost taste it. I immediately do not trust whatever resides inside this hut and begin making my way as far around it as I can. Then, the front door—the only door—starts to open.

I run as fast as I can to the other side of the clearing and back into the woods before the creature can see me, or I it. I do not want to face whatever it is with that amount of power while having no access to my own. Many beings dwell in these woods and most of them are blood thirsty.

Not for the first time since I left, I curse myself for not bringing anything with me; a knife, at the very least, would be helpful. The full gravity of my situation has started to sink in. I will need to sleep soon and figure out a way to feed myself. Any number of things from my room would have been useful right now.

Two more full nights passed before I finally stood before the Nocturia Mountains. I take very few breaks and sleep for an hour or two at a time. I still have yet to eat, which is beginning to take a toll on me. For nearly the entirety of this night, I travel uphill; every hour, my journey grows steeper. Climbing these cliff faces is not something I look forward to, particularly being as tired and hungry as I am.

It's another two nights before I find the entrance to a cave deep enough to hide away in. While fae do not need to eat, without access to my power I feel myself growing weaker every minute—food will slow it down. At least

I will be able to sleep here, and that sounds better than anything at the moment.

The cave is larger than it appeared when I first entered. The further back I go, the larger it becomes and the higher the ceilings are. There is a mineral or rock all throughout the cave that glows a bright blue and illuminates my surroundings perfectly.

"Do you make it a habit of entering the homes of others uninvited, boy?" A gravelly voice from somewhere within the cave asks, the echoes making it impossible to pinpoint an exact location.

"I did not know a cave could belong to any one being." I will not apologize for entering his "home"—a cave can be home to many and never belongs to one individual. The power that fills the cave from this being came on suddenly. It must have been dampened. If it's meant to give me a fright, it does not work. I am too tired to fear anything at the moment, and very soon my body is going to demand sleep, removing the choice from me entirely.

"Hmm, you are either very brave or very stupid. Which is it, boy?" Being called "boy" is beginning to wear on my nerves. I may not be grown, but I am no "boy" either.

"Neither—I am tired. I have been running for several nights, so it seems you will have a guest whether either of us like it." I am too tired to question the intelligence of my response. Luckily the being barks out a laugh and the power within the cave dampens again.

"I live here to avoid unexpected visitors. What is it that sent you running all the way up here into the mountains?" His tone has changed and he seems to have deemed me not to be a threat.

"My father, the King of the Night Court," I reply, making my way further back towards where the voice seems to be coming from. I spot the warm glow of a fire and follow it until I come upon an old male with long graying hair and a matching beard. He wears strange markings all over his face in what looks like blue ink.

"And what is it your father has done?" the male asks. I raise my hand to allow the light from the fire to glint on the red metal wrapped around my finger.

"He enslaved me with this damned thing over a decade ago, taking away my autonomy and stealing my power from me nightly. I cannot remove it. I have tried everything. This thing blocks me from accessing my own power." The male grows unnaturally still as he stares at my hand with the offending piece of metal.

"Where did you get that?" The way he asks makes the hairs on the back of my neck rise.

"My father tricked me into allowing him to slip it on my finger when I was nine." Such a fool I had been.

"Where did he get it?" he asks, still in that deadpan gaze like an animal getting ready to attack.

"I have not the slightest clue. The only thing I know is he said 'the whispers' inside his head told him where to go to find it, among other things. My father is insane. He has complete conversations with the voices inside his head, and his grasp on reality is non-existent." I think I will always carry the fear of the same illness rotting my mind. He makes a sound of acceptance, my answer passing whatever test he was giving me.

"You wish to have it removed?"

"More than anything," I say honestly. There is nothing I crave more in this realm, and once I am rid of the damned thing, I will never allow another to control me ever again.

"Come, sit. I know how to remove it," he says, like it's the easiest thing to do. What are the chances I would find the key to my true freedom all the way up here in the mountains? I take the seat he points to and watch as he picks up the largest blade I have ever seen.

"I have tried cutting it off more times than I can count." My excitement wanes knowing a knife will not work.

"This sword will. It can cut through anything, even magic." He sounds so sure of himself, it's hard not to let the excitement creep back in.

"What kind of magic is it?" After all of my years of searching, I never did find the answer to that question.

"One that has not been used in a millennium at least. And, should no longer still exist. Place your hand on this rock. This may hurt," he says as he severs my hand from my body. The pain is there, but I am overwhelmed with the euphoria rushing through me. The wall around my power and magic dissolves, allowing me to feel whole for the first time in more than half my life.

I am free.

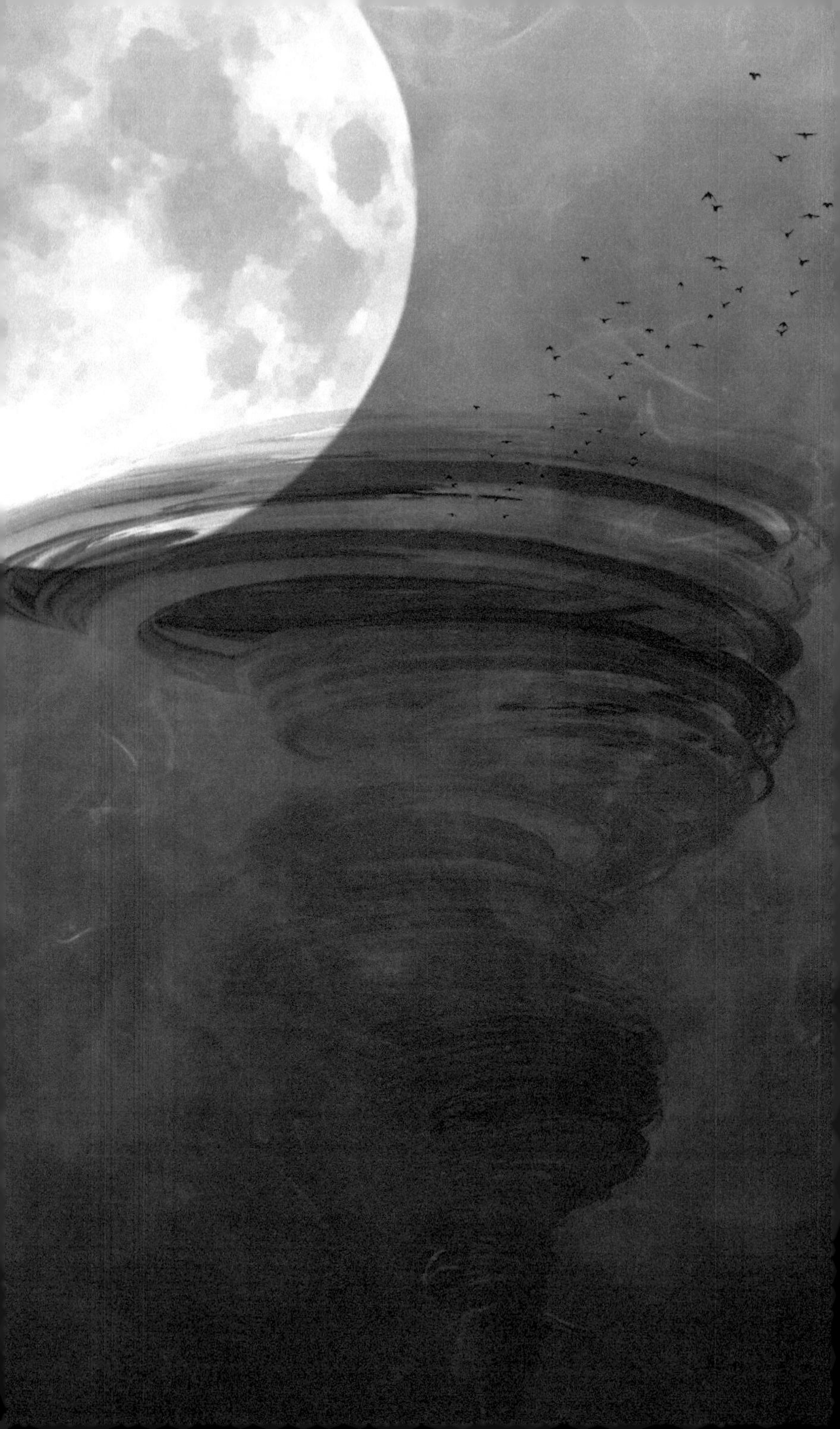

Six

KES

29 Years Old

For nine years I managed to survive the Night Court alone. I have been able to avoid the notice of my uncle, and rarely do I leave my chambers. It feels strange being alone here without my mother. I can now port anywhere I want within the chambers since the wards she placed ended when her life did. I still find myself porting into the parlor first, only now there is no one who checks on my comings and goings.

I have not gotten rid of her things—*their* things—yet, I am not sure I ever will. They act as a reminder that my parents existed. I can barely remember my father, and I know the day will come when my mother is nothing more than a faded memory lost to time. Keeping this place just the way it was when she left it for the last time makes me feel like I can preserve her memory. I know I am being ridiculous.

I did try to make the space my own. I'm tired of being haunted by the memories of what once was, yet I find it difficult to part with anything. I even tried rearranging things around, but every new configuration looks awkward, and in the end, I always return everything to their original positions. I think I would rather be haunted by memories than not all.

On the rare occasion I do leave my chambers, it's typically to hunt down more books showcasing different forms and strategies of the art of battle. I have done nothing but train my body and mind, preparing for the night my uncle remembers I exist.

While I have become as competent as one can teaching themselves, my skills have never been truly tested. Since my mother's death, the torment I receive from the court has changed. The reaction I had toward her headless body resulted in most of the court staying far away from me.

Not until a little over a year ago, when my wings started to fill out and I grew several inches, did the altercations resume with a few of the more vicious fae. I try to avoid any kind of violence with them, but it's becoming difficult to keep my mouth shut. It gets me into more trouble than anything else lately.

I do not care.

Even though my wings and taloned feet feel too big and cumbersome for my body, I am able to move with newfound grace. Every time I face off with a fae who seems to think I am easy pickings, I am often rewarded with a look of surprise when they realize, too late, they do not stand a chance against me.

Just last night, I was in the library when a burly fae with an ugly twisted face attempted to trip me as I walked back to the table I occupied. "Tried" being the key word.

My wings might be heavy, but I have learned to use them to offset any of my body's awkwardness that still persists.

I flared them open just enough to catch myself, barely showing any sign I tripped at all. I took a second to arrange an amused grin on my face and allowed my body to relax into the casual indifference I have been perfecting over the years. I noticed beings tend to mirror the reactions they get from me. If I show anger, they use their own anger to become defensive, and I prefer they feel a false sense of superiority.

"Well, hello there!" I gave the disgusting male a dazzling smile. "You seem to have misplaced your foot. Luckily, I found it for you." I find the more dramatic and theatrical I behave, the more confused the other fae become. This one was exceptionally slow. He stared at me for a moment too long with his mouth gaping open. It did not help his already unfortunate features.

"Shall I come back later, after you have located your voice as well? What do you say we meet back here tomorrow? Same time?" Ah, there it is. The fae, whose skin was already a bright red, was slowly turning a deep purple as he realized I called him slow. This is quickly becoming one of my favorite pastimes.

Normally, it's hard to tell if they are going to attempt to spar verbally before getting physical; however, in this case, the creature was an obvious idiot. There was no way, in any realm, he was going to come up with more than a couple grunted words. Something like, "trash" or my personal favorite, "bird." I could not for the life of me understand why anyone thought that was an insult. I am, quite literally, part bird.

His body moved almost as slowly as his brain, making his fists easy to dodge. This only proved to increase his anger, and his face turned a deeper shade of purple. I wonder, is it possible for one's head to explode from anger alone?

"You may want to calm down a fraction. If it's possible for a head to burst, I do believe you are well on your way." He roared and came at me with, what could be considered, speed. "This is your last chance to walk away. Think of what your friends will say when they discover you were beaten to a pulp by the likes of me. Save yourself the embarrassment, good sir!"

As I thought he would, he increased his effort, and like I warned him I would, I beat him to a pulp. The first strike is always the funniest to me. I live for that moment when it dawns on my opponent they are in way over their heads. Their eyes always go wide with their mouths shaped into O's. It never occurred to them: I looked like a threat, because I *am* a threat.

They are always too easy and untrained. I never once have had to use anything more than the basic moves I have known since I was a boy. I long to test out any of the skills I have taught myself which is why, even though I had been in many altercations, I still felt untested.

"Well, this has been a great time, but I really must be going. Send a scroll next time you want to hang out." I looked down on the male and gave him another one of my blinding smiles, making sure to show as many of my pointed teeth as possible. I even threw in a jaunty little wink.

The teeth are another new development. Over the last few years, I've been losing my flat teeth and, much to my delight, they have been replaced by a mouthful of razor sharp points. I imagine they make my theatrics even more disconcerting.

I am not surprised by the scroll that appears in front of me, demanding my presence at one of the many training facilities in the palace. I knew my antics were bound to place me front and center of the king's attention at some point. I am honestly surprised it has taken as long as it has since Ciaran escaped in the middle of second night. His father had been in a full rage for three years following his disappearance. From all accounts, he was behaving like a wild animal. He scratched and clawed at his skin, demanding his son be found. Until one day he just stopped looking, and his wild behaviors ended at the same time.

Now that the time has come, I do not know if I could ever be truly ready to meet face to face with my uncle. At least it's not a summons to the throne room. With no more time to waste, I take a deep breath and port to a training room of the king's choice.

"Nephew, I do not enjoy being kept waiting," the king says with contempt. This is already going great. Out of habit I fall into my relaxed stance and give the king one of my shining smiles. The annoyance he wears on his face quickly slips into anger. This is going *really* great.

"My apologies. I was at one of those parts in a book where it's impossible to put it down. Great book – I can lend it to you when I am finished." Why the fuck did I just say that?

"I see you have your father's mouth. Perhaps, I can break you of it yet. You see, Kes, I am in need of an heir, and since you are the only prince in the palace, I have decided you shall be my successor." That's a load of shit. There is no way he would ever want me on the throne, not when Ciaran is still out there somewhere.

"While I appreciate the offer, I have no interest in the throne." Gods, why do I keep letting stupid thoughts leave my lips? There is no way I'm making it out of here alive.

"Did I ask if you wanted it? You *will* be the next in line, and you *will* be trained the way Ciaran should be getting trained. I will not have a weak heir. I hear you have been picking fights with members of my court." I notice he says "my" and not "the" or "our." He truly feels like it all belongs to him and him alone.

"I would hardly call any of those 'fights.' I was simply making new friends. Although, I will say, I do not think any of them are keen to see me again." I wink. I winked at the king...death is imminent.

To my surprise, he begins to laugh. A deep rumbling belly laugh. I have never seen the king laugh before, and it's rather unsettling. Is this a good sign or a bad sign? Likely bad, I do not think the king has anything good in mind for anyone.

"Let's see if you keep your father's mouth at the end of this training. Your instructors will be many." This piques my interest; I will not say no to actual training. "Their method is unusual-however, I do believe it will have the desired effect." No less than twenty fae step out from the shadows, all of them moving with a grace that speaks of centuries of training. The way they look at me and the way the king's face split into a knowing grin makes me nervous.

"How kind of you—looks like you really splurged on me." At this point I know nothing good is coming. I decided to really go for it and elevate my performance.

"You could say that. What you see are twenty-three of the court's finest warriors. They will all be training you...at the same time. Perhaps a group effort will break you of your wagging tongue." Fuck. This is not going to go well for me. Two or three, maybe I could hold my own long enough to take a decent beating. Twenty? I will be lucky if I survive. No matter what happens, I will never give the king the satisfaction of my silence.

"Well," I say with a dramatic pause, "that certainly is not conventional, I will give you that. When does this party begin?" I mime a little dance just to really push him over the edge as I subtly prepare my body for pain. I have felt psychological pain and mild physical pain, however, this—there is no preparing for the agony waiting for me at the hands of twenty-three fae warriors.

"Now." The king laughs maniacally as a wall of fae prowls towards me. Each of them takes their time, likely to intimidate me. It's definitely working, but I cannot let them or the king know it.

"What? No dinner first? I have never had so many eyes looking at me with such hunger. I would have worn something nicer. I honestly cannot blame you—I mean, have you seen me?" Several of their lips twitch while even more scowl. Adrenaline pumps through my veins, and even though I know this will likely kill me, being able to finally test my skills thrills me.

"Finally," I say, giving them all a huge smile, showing off as many of my sharp teeth as I can.

"Awe, look! The little rooster has teeth." There is a low murmur of laughter.

"Oh, yes!" I exclaim. "They are new—do you like them?" This time when I smile, it's not fake enthusiasm. I am truly excited by the impending violence.

"I do," the male who called me "little rooster" says. "I am going to make sure I have all of them before we are finished." With that, they all pounce.

I held my own for a while. Well, maybe more like a short period of time, but in that time I see approval flash in several of their eyes. It's not much longer, and I am in a bloody heap on the floor—all of my teeth are indeed missing.

"Bravo!" The king exclaims, while slowly clapping. I can barely see through the swelling around my eyes that is already setting in. The king comes to stand before my mangled body and squats down, looking me in the eyes.

"This will happen *every* time you disrespect me. If you wish to avoid it, keep your mouth shut from now on." He smiles, clearly pleased with himself.

"Now, *that* was a party." I say, the words sounding strange between my missing teeth and swelling lips. I give him a gummy, bloody smile and try to wink at him again. I hear a quiet smattering of laughter that quickly turns into throat clearing when the king stands and whips his head towards the culprits.

"We will see about that," he says as I start laughing. I hear him growl before I see him pull his booted foot back and swing it towards my head. That is the last thing I remember. Everything goes black and oblivion welcomes me into her waiting arms.

SEVEN

CIARAN

35 Years Old

The sword is unnaturally heavy. If I were any smaller, I would not be able to lift, let alone wield, such a weapon. It fights me every time I hold it, making it even harder to train with. Master Ulgridge says the sword was created specifically for him by fate, and it tends to ensure difficulties for anyone else who attempts to pick it up. If it were not for his mastery of skill with the blade, and his willingness to train me, I would never call him "Master" anything.

According to him, it does not "fight" me. It's "annoyed" to be in my hands and makes it "merely difficult." Since he handed it to me himself, I am able to train with it, as opposed to if I pick it up on my own. I did not believe him, until I tried for myself. It was… impossible. If I wished it to go one way, it went the other, while also somehow making itself even heavier. He refuses to tell me how he really came into possession of it, but continues to tell me the same story every time I ask.

It's a fine sword—better than fine. I have never seen a metal like the one the blade has been forged from. Sometimes, when Master Ulgridge wields it, I am almost certain I see a blue light surrounding it; however, before I can be sure, it disappears. The blade itself is only a couple heads smaller than I am, requiring me to use my now fully grown wings as a counter balance.

He assures me learning to wield a weapon as difficult as his will only make me more proficient with a lesser one. I am not complaining, the physical strength the blade requires from me has only made the slender frame of youth expand into the nearly grown male I am tonight. I have never felt more capable in my life. I would like to see my father try and control me now.

It has taken me several years to become even mildly acceptable with the unruly blade. I still find it cumbersome and awkward to move. I am far more skilled at avoiding its kiss when Ulgridge has me at the end of his blade. In the beginning, he had to pull back at the last second to avoid dismembering me—again.

Several years ago, he was training me to dodge his blade, when I suddenly moved at an unnatural speed—a skill puberty has gifted me. I can move from one place to another almost as fast as I can port.

I created a game I am rather fond of with Master Ulgridge. If I move quietly and quickly enough while he's distracted, I can catch him unaware. He's not as much of a fan of my game as I am, even though, so far, he has always heard me coming.

He can hear the most minuscule of sounds. He says he can hear the trees at the foot of these mountains blow in the breeze. I would be less likely to believe him if he had not been able to hear me coming every time, or when he instructs me to go take down one of the birds flying overhead... while we are in the depths of the cave. He has never been wrong.

Frustrated by my clumsiness, I toss the blade to the ground. He gives me one of his looks of disapproval I have begun to detest. I would not say I care for him, however, for some reason, I care a great deal what he thinks of me. We have built a type of mutual respect between us, one which I have never shared with another. The type of relationship I had once craved from my father.

What a stupid boy I had been. If I ever see my father again, I *will* get my revenge. I reach into my pocket and touch the ring I once wore like a shackle, allowing my father complete control over everything but my mind. The moment I see my father again, he will get the chance to know what it feels like to be controlled.

It would not be to the same degree to which he had once controlled me, unfortunately. As soon as Master Ulgridge severed my hand, he somehow removed the offending magic from it, returning it to its original state. Still a magical ring, just no longer infused with the magic he still refuses to tell me about. Where it had once been the deepest of reds, it was now a metal of the lightest tone, nearly white.

While it could still control a being, it was far less nefarious. The ring will now give the individual who places it upon another's finger the ability to block their power and cause them to freeze in place at any time. Unfortunately, both effects only last an hour at most. At least it remains impossible for the ring to be removed by anyone besides the being who places it on the finger to begin with.

It was not the severity I wished for, yet it would still provide my father with a small taste of the torture he put me through. I am certain I can come up with other ways to make his life the abomination he once made mine. I will make him beg me for death.

Master Ulgridge picks up his sword and points it at me, a silent command to ready myself. He somehow manages to command me while making it not seem like a command. However he does it, he has figured out how to communicate to me without sending me into a fit of rage. The first time I had to leave the mountain to speak with another fae, their tone set me off and was ultimately the cause of their demise. It was a shame, too, because I did not get the information I sought.

He begins swinging the large sword with a familiarity forged through time, or perhaps fate. I cannot say I do not find his story mildly believable. Fate has a way of getting what it wants, and if what it wants is to have a specific sword in a specific being's hands, that is exactly what will happen. Besides, I cannot come up with a better theory for the sword's perplexing behavior.

I dodge the blade with growing ease. The "whoosh" of his blade cutting the air and the ambient noises of the cave are the only sounds heard while we glide through our dance. Majority of the time we live in the near silence around us. Neither of us desire to speak, with the exception of when Ulgridge gives a quick correction. Or even less often, when he tells me one of the fantastical stories he created of far away lands.

"There is a place called the Realm of Gods," he says, abruptly beginning one of his stories. How he comes up with them, I will never know. He has never mentioned this "Realm of Gods" before, yet I am sure it will be entertaining—he's an exceptional storyteller. My silence is enough for him to continue on with his tale.

"The Realm of Gods is made up of many different territories, what you would call courts," he starts while I continue to duck and weave away from the blade, which never slows its pursuit of me. "There is the Yggdrasil territory, where the entire land is made up of one giant tree." I look at him disbelieving, this may be one of the most fantastical stories he has told yet. My pause almost cost me an injury.

"There are nine realms within the tree and the gods reside in the uppermost realm, Asgard. If you wish to enter or leave Asgard you must first pass a single guard and traverse the Bifrost Bridge. The all-seeing and all-hearing guard is the only watchman for the entire realm of Asgard." A tree, a bridge, and possibly the most unbelievable part of his story—a single guard. If he saw the look I gave him again, he did not acknowledge it. Instead, he switches his attack, causing me to stumble while I attempt to keep up.

"There is one god who defies the watchman, he's a trickster and sneaks past the guard often, coming and going as he sees fit. The guard can see throughout all of the lands of Yggdrasil. And it's said his hearing is so great he can even hear the grass growing. How the trickster manages to avoid detection is a matter of much contempt for the guard." He's increasing the speed of his attack, causing me to move faster and faster. Ulgridge seemed to be growing angry over the story.

"Why does it matter if a god comes and goes?" I cannot help but ask, this story is ridiculous.

"It *matters,*" he says, sounding annoyed by what he clearly seems to think is a stupid question. "Because the gods have enemies, the Jotuns, and this trickster god happens to be part Jotun. He never shows true allegiance to the gods, and he's prone to theft of powerful objects. He claimed 'all in good fun,' yet the items he steals typically end up in the hands of the Jotuns.

"The guard alerts Asgard to any attacks coming from the Jotuns by blowing his horn, Gjallarhorn. He defends the bridge until the gods come down from Asgard, and together they fight back any threat. The guard is said to wield a great sword, Hofud—"

"Who has come up with these horrible names? Hofud is hardly terrifying," I say. I do not usually interrupt him this many times, but this story is unraveling quickly. He's usually far more entertaining, but this feels like one of the most obscure history texts I have ever encountered. Worse than some of my ancestor's journals. He stares at me for a few moments, and I stare back, before he attempts to remove my right arm with a swift swing of his blade. He obviously does not appreciate my commentary.

"*Hofud* is said to be sharp enough that it can cut through *anything*." His gaze lands on the blade as I spin to avoid it. I cannot help but follow his gaze. Surely he's not implying his masterpiece of a weapon is some fairytale sword. I roll my eyes at the ridiculous thought of anything so fine being named something so horrid—Hofud... sounds like someone has sneezed. I step off to the side, avoiding another swing of his blade.

"The guard is the god of order and stability, while this trickster god is born of chaos. One night, at a feast, the trickster was intoxicated and spewed insults at many of the gods attending the festivities. It would be one thing if the trickster were funny, but he's the equivalent of a bug that will not cease pestering your face. The two gods came to blows, over multiple instances, their relationship only worsening with the passing of time.

"The day came when the trickster did the unspeakable—he killed the guard's brother. His brother had been the kindest of the gods and was loved by all. The trickster had likely become jealous of the attention the favorite of the gods received. He slipped through the guard's unnaturally keen senses and disappeared.

"The gods searched all the realm for the trickster, never finding him. Instead, they found his children living with their witch mother, Angrboda, in the Ironwood forest. His children are monsters—a giant serpent, the largest wolf in all the realms, and a daughter. The daughter appeared normal enough until you looked closer—her legs held the flesh of the dead. She's an unnatural creature straddling the line of both the dead and the living." The way he speaks of the children bothers me; it's not their fault they were born the way they were. I move with all the speed I have to stand behind the old fae, causing him to spin and be caught off guard.

"The gods held the children in Asgard, hoping to draw the trickster out of hiding. The guard told them the trickster was nowhere in all the realms of Yggdrasil. He told them he was likely not in the Realm of Gods at all. No one would listen, however, since the trickster was known to avoid the guard's keen senses.

"Eventually the All-Father grew tired of waiting for his blood brother to show himself, and his children were proving to be difficult to detain. He eventually sent the half-dead daughter to rule over Helheim, the underworld. The serpent he banished to the oceans surrounding Midgard; it's said he's so long he encircles the entirety of the realm. The wolf proved to be the hardest to banish and eventually had to be tricked into being bound by chains on the Island of Lyngvi."

"Why were the children punished for the crimes of their father? Were they not living peacefully before the gods came to take them away?" A fairytale this might be—I could not help but find it fascinating. I found myself siding with the trickster; he sounded like any being of the Night Court.

"The children are foretold to be the harbingers of the end of the times." Unbelievably, he swung harder and faster at me, as if he could hear my thoughts and they made him angry.

"The guard grew wary of his post. There was no sign of the trickster and all was quiet in the realms, a sure sign he was nowhere within Yggdrasil. The All-Father told the guard it was time for him to go and experience the rest of the realms outside of their own lands. Enjoy time away to relax. Instead of doing what he suggested, the guard took it upon himself to search for the trickster throughout every realm outside the Realm of Gods.

"It's said, when the two see each other again, the guard will blow his horn and announce Ragnarök has arrived. The guard is intent on avoiding Ragnarök, and that is why he searches for the trickster. If he can find him before the other gods get a hold of him, he could kill him. With his death, perhaps Ragnarök will never come. He still searches to this night. He spends a millennium in each realm waiting to catch any hint of the trickster's meddling."

"Who guards the bridge with him gone?" It's always fun to ask these questions and see what tales he can come up with on the spot. He stops his swinging and appraises Ciaran for a moment.

"Time moves differently in each of the realms. In the Human Realm time moves the fastest, days going by in the time it takes for one full night to pass here. In the Realm of Gods time moves the slowest. The guard has been gone for what would be thousands upon thousands of years here for us, however, not even a day has passed there. Gods live forever. There is no need for days to go by quickly." It always amazes me how he can come up with something oddly logical so quickly.

"And what is this Ragnarök?" He spoke about it as though I should have prior knowledge of his imaginary world.

"The end of times. That is a story for another time." I think about the story he just shared, when it occurs to me—how would one random god have the senses he spoke of and not the others?

"How did this guard come to have such incredible hearing and sight?" There is no way he can easily come up with a quick answer for this one.

"He sacrificed a body part," he says, like it was the most obvious answer.

"What body part?" I ask, not satisfied with the answer he gave.

"His ear." That made me pause before looking over at Master Ulgridge and staring at his missing ear. I wondered, not for the first time, what happened to the absent appendage. Perhaps he draws upon real experiences to create his stories. I wonder if any of his stories hold any truth to them after all.

He does have excellent hearing.

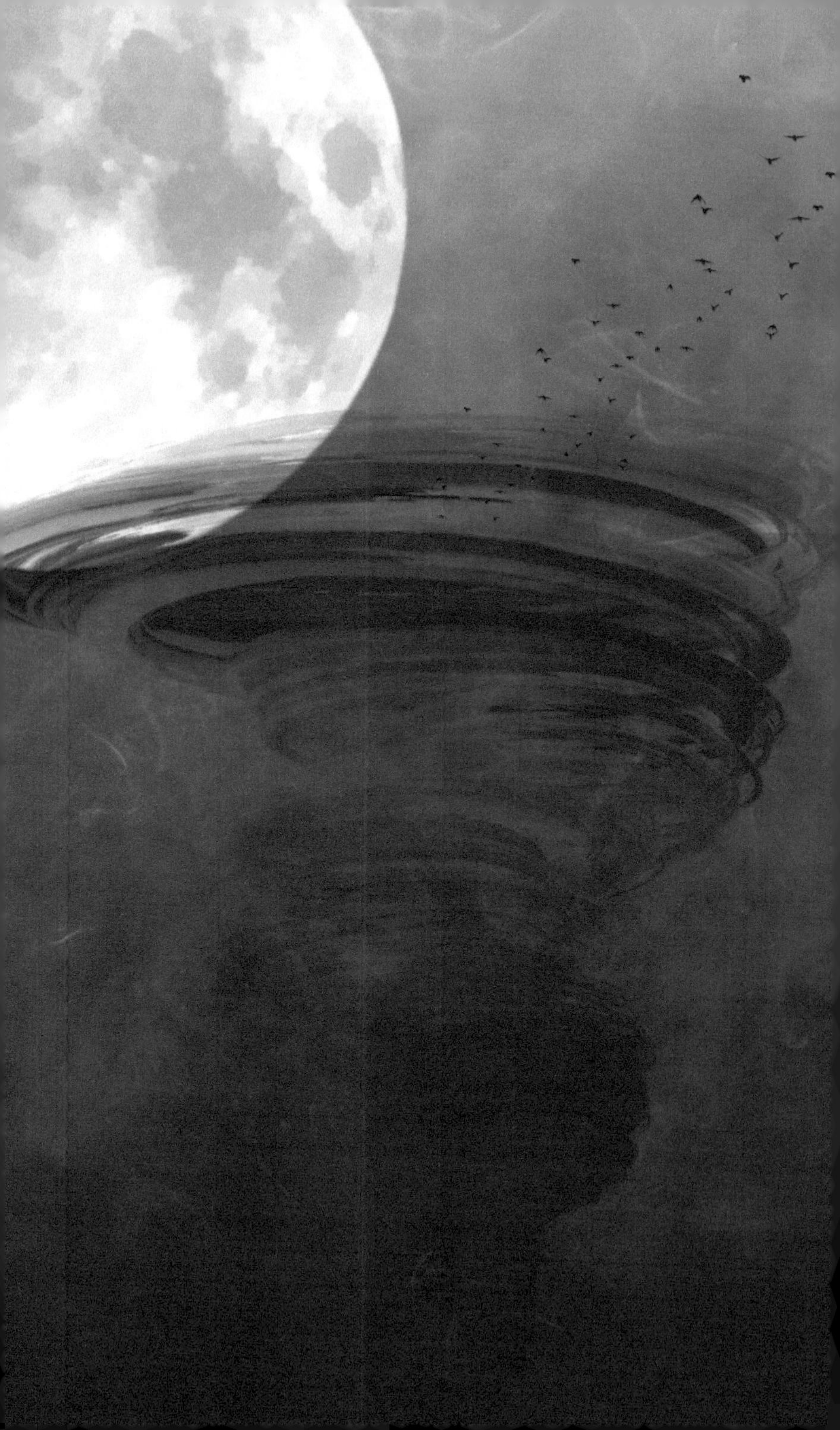

EIGHT

KES

47 Years Old

A hand is thrust into my face, an offering from Tani-ka, to help me to my feet. A few of the warriors responsible for my "training" began properly educating me over a decade ago. After beating me to a mushy lump of blood and feathers every few days, I started to become faster and stronger—even taking several of them down with me.

Tanika was the first to approach me outside of the "training" sessions. She said she could see real potential in the way I moved and with the right training I could be unstoppable. Apparently the "right training" also includes a different sort of combat; one without clothing and not within the walls of the training facility—most of the time.

She's the first female I ever fucked, and while we still do, she's no longer the only one. There is nothing between us besides a need for release, and what she can teach to mold me into a powerful weapon. She still beats the shit out of me with the others when my uncle demands it. She always wears a smile on her face while doing it, too.

It was not long before others joined us to pound their knowledge into me, both metaphorically and literally. Most of them train me in either hand-to-hand or weapons combat. I am becoming rather adept with a sword.

However, it's Mondost I look forward to training with the most. Like me, he has the elemental air and has shown me how to use it in conjunction with my body to attack. I am becoming rather fond of taking the air directly from my opponents lungs. Still clumsy when trying to do both, I find it difficult to think of everything at the same time with the speed he demands of me.

"You still pause when attacking from your left. You may as well announce your plans to the entire realm." Tanika picked up on my tells early on and loves to use them to knock me down whenever I give away my next move.

"Ah, you have it all wrong, mighty little cherub," she hates it when I call her that, so I make sure to do it as often as possible. "I am simply pausing for dramatic effect." I give her a theatrical bow and smile when I hear her make several noises of annoyance.

"Kes, be serious. You need to learn to stop letting your foes know where you are going next." This is one thing I do not like about her—she has no patience for any of my antics and does not contain the wit to verbally spar. It's her only flaw, but it's a rather large one, and it makes her quite dull in my opinion.

"But... but..." I stick my lower lip out at her in a mockery of a pout. Another thing I do she hates, but when I get her riled up like this, she gives herself away worse than I do. She has very little control of her rage, and I am certain it will be the end of her some night. I make sad little noises I know will annoy her further as I see her get ready to come at me. She always drops her right shoulder before she hits in anger, allowing me to catch her arm, pull, and flip her to the ground.

"Who is announcing their next move now? Awe, the mighty little cherub is also mighty in her rage." I place my hand in her face to offer the same assist she just offered to me. She slaps it away, just as I knew she would, and picks herself up. I cannot help but laugh at her. Her violet skin turns nearly blue when she gets angry.

"Kes, if you do not start taking this seriously, you will not survive the years to come!" she yells at me. No one seems to understand that I am always serious, I just do not project it outwardly. You would think Tanika, of all beings, would know with as much time we have spent togeth-er over the years. My theatrical nature is confusing, and rather unsettling, to most members of the Night Court. It's something I have nearly perfected, and I enjoy using it to my advantage.

"You wound me, mighty one! How dare you think I do not take this seriously!" I say in mock offense. This will likely be her last shred of patience.

"I am going to enjoy beating the piss out of you later!" she screams in my face.

"Ouch! I am truly heartbroken," I say with an exagger-ated frown. She huffs and storms away as I laugh hyster-ically. "Just do not let your shoulder drop!" This elicits a scream from behind her teeth, and I laugh even harder.

Since I now have mutual respect with several of the "trainers" my uncle chose for me, they give me a warning on the nights he decides I need to be reminded of my place. He refuses to give up on his quest to make me his heir.

Lately, he has even begun trying to pit me against my cousin in the most ridiculous ways. He tries to make me jealous of him, which is hard to do when the other being has not been around for quite some time. He tries to make me despise him, however, in the process he only succeeds in doing the opposite. While my hate for him may be waning, I do *not* care for him. He will always be the one who killed my mother.

After being subjected to his father's ministrations for so long, I can understand why a youngling with so little years behind him could succumb to the manipulations of such a vile being. It's clear the king is mad. Over the years I have witnessed him having one-sided conversations and arguments with himself, and have heard him mention *the whispers* in his head.

A mad king is worse than a wicked king; there is no reasoning with a mad king. Many fae have lost their heads trying to reason with the unreasonable. He has taken to beheading his victims whom he claims to be "traitors" now that Ciaran has left. It's the most bizarre thing to watch—the extreme pleasure he takes in the killing of our own kind. He throws his head back and releases a moan of pleasure. Bizarre indeed, and rather disturbing.

As if thoughts of my uncle have summoned him, a spelled scroll appears in front of my face demanding my presence in the very training facility I have been in all day. It's always the same one, and I have taken to referring to it as "my" training arena. I like to think of it as an arena on the nights I am forced to take on all twenty-three warriors at once. It's always a spectacle; I make sure of it.

My uncle tries to beat my "father's mouth" out of me, and has failed more times than I can count. I think it's an unfair observation, because I clearly have my own sharp tongue and I barely remember my father. Either way, all his abuse does is push me to see how much more ridiculous I can get with him. I will be honest, it's becoming harder to be more theatrical than I already am.

"I see you have learned not to keep me waiting." My uncle's abrasive voice comes from the shadowed corner of the room, the same place he stands every time we do this. He still likes for the twenty-three to come out from the shadows at one time, and seems to think I find it intimidating. I find it uninspiring.

"Oh, look! It's my dear uncle. Did you bring along your little invisible friend again? Where are they? Are they there beside you? Hello, my uncle's invisible friend—how kind of you to join us. I am sure it will be quite the spectacle." There was nothing, and I mean *nothing*, that made my uncle angrier. I learned a while ago he would never kill me and risk leaving no heir to the throne. He would never allow his legacy to be an empty throne.

"Nephew, I see that mouth of yours has yet to improve. Ciaran would not lower himself to such antics. I cringe at the king you would make." He still thinks he can convince me to be his heir, but even more ridiculous are his horrible attempts to incite jealousy or competition in me against my absent cousin. Not only is the king insane, he's also... well... stupid.

"Oh, my sweet, precious uncle. I know aging is difficult, but you really must remember I have no desire to be king, and I am definitely nowhere near jealous of my cousin. He has the personality of a rock. Honestly, that might even be too kind. I think a rock has a wider range of expression than that of your offspring." I clasp my hands together and hold them under my chin while looking at him as if he were the most adorable creature in the realm.

He started aging recently. His once jet black, oil sheen hair has been invaded by an army of little white strands. The skin on his face, once perfectly smooth, now holds the beginning of creases. I liked to remind him of it as often as possible. It's a welcome reminder to me that he will not live forever.

I can see the exact moment his anger becomes a living beast inside him. Finally, the party is about to get started. I learned a few new tricks over the past several nights, and

I have a tingling under my skin in anticipation of testing them out. My feathers even raise a bit. I wonder if it makes me look adorably fluffy or intimidatingly larger. I like to think it's a combination of the two. How terrifying that must appear.

"One of these nights you will take such a horrific beating, you will never open your mouth to spew such youngish behavior again. You will fall in line and take your place as my heir, like the pet bird you are." I do enjoy a good bird joke, but that was just lazy; he should be embarrassed. He snaps his fingers, enjoying his own flair for dramatics, and the twenty-three emerge from the shadows.

"It's lovely you hang on to these dreams of yours, Uncle. However, I think we are both aware my tongue will only grow sharper. You must know, I really do enjoy these 'trainings' of yours—they are so very dramatic." Without taking my eyes off of my uncle, I watch the twenty-three begin to close in around me. I have quite the show planned for tonight. My smile is filled with true joy that shows off every single one of my razor sharp teeth. I wink at my uncle. He *really* hates that.

The first wave advances and I am able to keep the upper hand while several of them lay on the floor around me. As they get up, the next wave arrives. I fight them all, knocking fewer down as I start to take hit after hit. I see out of the corner of my eye my uncle wearing that smug expression he dons every time he thinks he has won.

I flair my wings out wide and flap them while using my power to stir up the air around me. I catch a grin gracing Mondost's face as I start to spin, taking the surrounding air with me. I gain speed, spinning faster and faster, as I raise up a few feet within the cyclone I have created. I can see my uncle gripping on to the wooden beam next to him. It's a sight I will never forget.

As soon as I gain my desired momentum, I come to a sudden stop and throw the air out around me, sending every single being flying into the walls around us, including my uncle. Before I am able to gloat, I hear a voice behind me as I am taken to the ground.

"You really need to stop projecting your next move." I laugh hysterically while the twenty-three beat me into the inevitable bloody mess I was destined for.

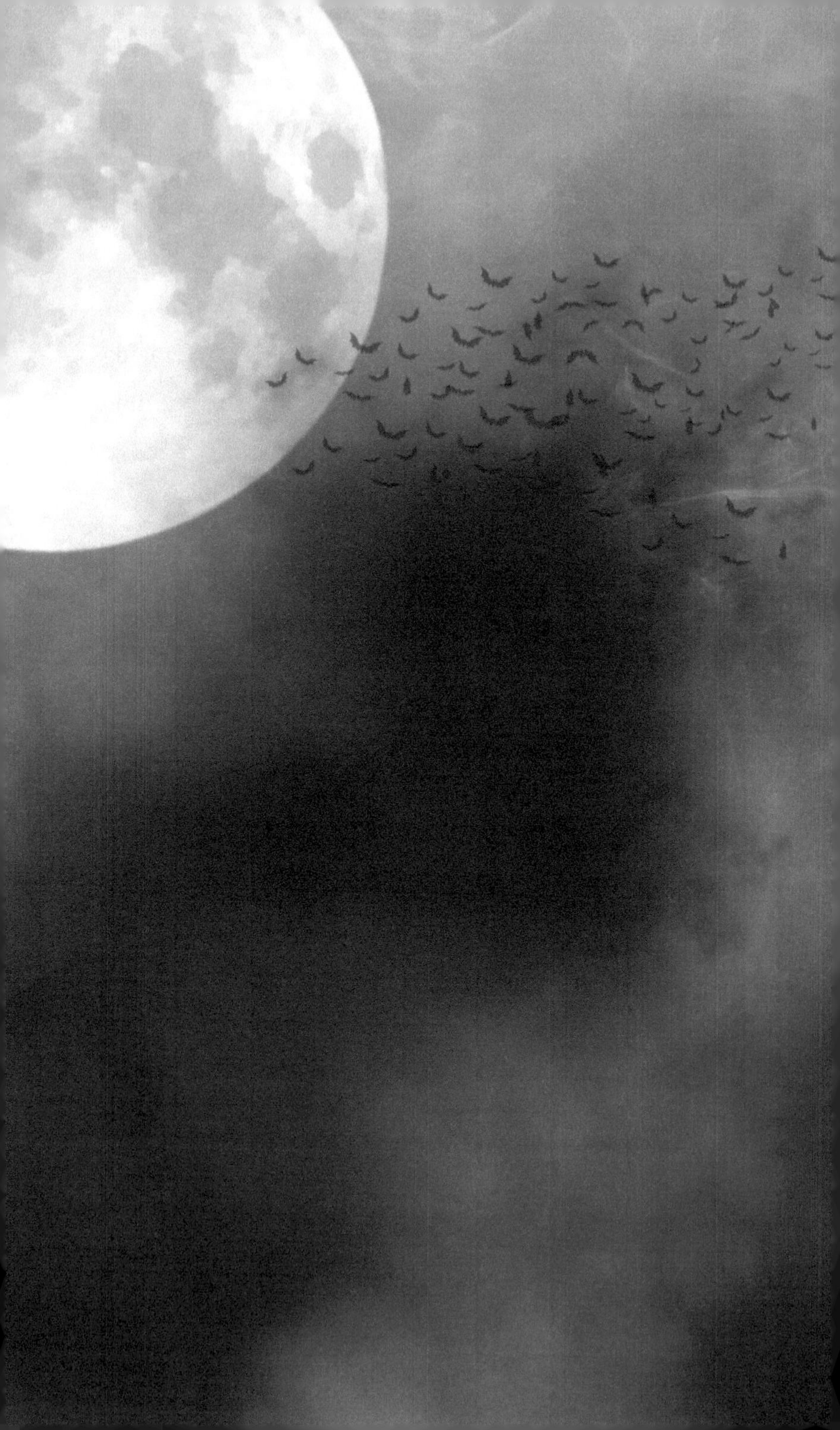

Nine

CIARAN

62 Years Old

I have been following this particular Night fae for several hours now. Ulgridge wants to find the origin of the ring that once adorned my finger, and I am inclined to help him. I would love to pay the creatures who had a hand in my enslavement a visit and let them know, intimately, the lasting impact it made on me.

He's sent me out to track down specific beings. He says he hears certain things through the realm, then he follows the information until it leads back to a particular fae. This one is the dealer of the original spelled ring I now carry in my pocket. I want to know whose hands it landed in next.

The city of Lunarmist is far smaller than Nightfell, however, that does not mean it's truly a small place. Fae of all shapes and sizes move throughout the busy streets from one storefront to another. The male I am following is a dealer of magical objects, and a popular one at that. Every other being he passes stops to share a few brief words before moving on, making it difficult to find my window of opportunity.

Outside the city, I have a work table and the roll of tools I have collected over the years set up. It's a magnificent spot; you can see the falls off in the distance, and the sound will muffle the screams. As soon as he gives me the opening I need, I will port us to my makeshift workstation where we can have a private *conversation*.

Finally, the male turns down a deserted alleyway. I see my chance and take it. One moment the male is whistling some off-pitch tune and the next I have him strapped to my table. He blinks rapidly while his mind attempts to catch up to his sudden change in scenery. He takes a few moments longer to notice the restraints holding him down.

"Wh—what is the meaning of this!" the male rages. He pulls several times on his bonds, the chains clanking together in a perverse melody. "Unhand me this minute! Do you have any idea who I am?" He does not notice me standing at the foot of the table yet.

"I believe the more pertinent question is, do you not know who I am?" I ask, moving into his line of sight. I know I look a great deal like my father; my glowing golden eyes are the only things I inherited from my mother. I am certain hers glowed at some point in her life, though I never saw them.

The male stares at me for a long moment, trying to piece together who I am. I watch his thoughts as each one flits across his mind. He knows I am not my father, and a long time has passed since anyone has seen the true heir of the Night Court. I smile my extra-wide smile the moment he realizes with whom he speaks.

"You are the prince," he says in a quiet voice—shocked. "You have grown into quite the fae, prince. What can I do for you? Are these chains necessary?" I can practically hear the wheels turning in his brain as he begins piecing a plan together to survive this encounter.

"Not particularly, I suppose. That is if you give me all of the information I seek. I will say, I will be rather put out if you do. I did set this all up, just for you, after all. I would hate for it to be wasted." I will not let him go even if he tells me what I want to know freely. He has seen my face and I do not want word to travel throughout the court about sightings of the missing prince. Besides, I have been looking forward to this part all night long.

"What is it you wish to know, prince? I am sure we can get this sorted quickly and not waste more of each other's time." He must think I am stupid. Not once has he addressed me as "*my* prince," and I did not miss the insinuation that I am the one wasting his time. I laugh darkly and watch the male second guess his choice of words.

Too late.

"I am not sure if I am more insulted or thrilled by your disrespect." He tries to interrupt me with a frantic apology but keeps tripping over his own words.

"Hush now. There is still the matter of the information you have that I want." He calms a bit and listens intently; there is still hope swirling in his eyes. He thinks he's walking away from this.

"Of course, my prince. What is it you seek?" I chuckle again at his attempt to rectify his earlier choices. Pulling the ring out of the pocket I have kept it in all of these years, I hold it over his face. Twisting it in the moonlight, I give him a clear view of it.

"This ring was once in your possession and you sold or traded it to another. I want to know who." I snapped the ring away from his face, keeping it in my hand.

"I do not know. I cannot be certain what ring that is. It looks like many rings I have traded throughout my thousands of years as a dealer." He's lying.

Wonderful.

"I find that hard to believe. I have seen several fine pieces in my short existence and I have never seen a metal as close to white like the one this ring is made from. Perhaps you do not remember and you need a little refresher on this particular piece." The second I grab his hand, he starts to fight against me; he knows exactly what ring this is. I shove the ring on his finger and the man gasps as he feels the spell worm its way through his veins. Sadly, it does not look even a fraction as painful as it was when the ring was placed on my finger.

"I think you lied to me...what do you think?" I ask, as I unroll the leather carrying case with all of my toys across his chest.

"N—no, or, or at least it was not my intention, my prince." What a sad excuse for a Night fae. His whole body begins to shake and it rattles my tools. I sigh and give him a disapproving look.

"I understand, however, I now have a dilemma. How am I to believe anything that spews from your lips? You already proved to be a liar and attempted to conceal the information I desire." His shaking is starting to anger me. I slap him across the face and bring my own down to hover above his.

"Get a hold of yourself, you coward!" I yell into his face, causing his eyes to bulge wide. "Stop. Shaking." I hiss through my teeth before pulling away. He nods his head vigorously and tries to control himself. He's still trembling, but a mere fraction of what he had been.

"Good. I would hate to have to use the ring to freeze you in place. Waiting for the spell to wear off to allow you to speak again would make me rather furious." I stare into his eyes before cocking my head to the side and say, "You do not want to make me furious." He shakes his head in agreement.

"Would you like a second attempt to tell me the truth about the ring?" The male hesitates before he sighs and nods his head.

"I did not want to tell you, not because I do not remember, but because of who I traded with. It was...it was a Day fae." He flinches as the words leave him.

"Let me get this straight. You traded a ring, as powerful as this, directly into the hands of our enemies? Did you not consider the possibility it could wind up on the finger of one of your own rulers?" If there was any shred of hope for this male living throughout the night, it's long gone now. As of now, he's destined to die under my hands before first night comes.

"No, he promised me it would not. When I trade things with him, he often trades equally dangerous items with me. He said something about a creature in the very south of the Day Court looking for something exactly like the ring. Since the south of the Day Court is nothing but lesser fae, I thought it would be harmless. He assured me it would never be used against the Night Court." He fully believes the words this Day fae trader spoke. What a fool.

"Well, he was obviously unable to promise such things considering by the time it wound up on my own finger, it had been mutated into something exceedingly worse." The male's eyes grow wide at my confession.

"Because of your actions, I was enslaved for over a decade. Now, do you not think you owe me the name of the Day fae you trade with?" His trembling is increasing, and I see the effort he puts into attempting to contain it.

"I do not know his name. We have never traded names. I can tell you where and when we meet. P-p-please, my prince, spare me," he stuttered.

"Where is this place, and when is your next meeting?" He freely gives me all of the details I need. I have a new life's mission to hunt down every last being responsible for this fucking ring finding its way into my father's hands.

"Good. That is good." I praise him and he melts to the table in relief. "When this ring," I take it off his finger and hold it back up to the moonlight, "found its way onto my finger, it acquired another spell. One that gives the being who places the ring on another's finger complete control over their body and access to their well of power, while blocking the wearer from accessing any of their own power or magic. Can you imagine having your body move and carry out actions without being the one to instruct your own limbs? My thoughts remained my own, however, this ring caused my own mind to feel like a prison. The things my father forced me to do." Returning the ring to the pocket it now lives in, I watch the trader's eyes grow wider than should be possible.

"I see you are surprised. The King of the Night Court somehow found the ring in his possession and used it on his own son, in his never ending quest for more power. He made me carry out every torture and execution of every fae he deemed a traitor, from the time I was nine until I finally got away at twenty. You can thank him for the skills I now have. I will be honest with you, it's the one thing I silently thank him for as well. I do enjoy my little hobby, even more now, since I am the one choosing what to carve next.

Lately, I have been working on my penmanship. Currently, it's still abysmal."

If the confessions did not convince him he will not survive the night, those last words should have. His death is going to be slow and painful. The cries for mercy begin, and as usual, it's a sound that grates in my ears and makes my teeth hurt. It does not matter though, because very soon his pleas will turn into the screams that I enjoy. I can change the tone of a scream by applying pain in certain ways and in certain places, playing my victims like some disturbing musical instrument.

I choose the smallest blade in the bundle. While it's the smallest, it's also the sharpest and perfect for practicing my letters. I begin to carve.

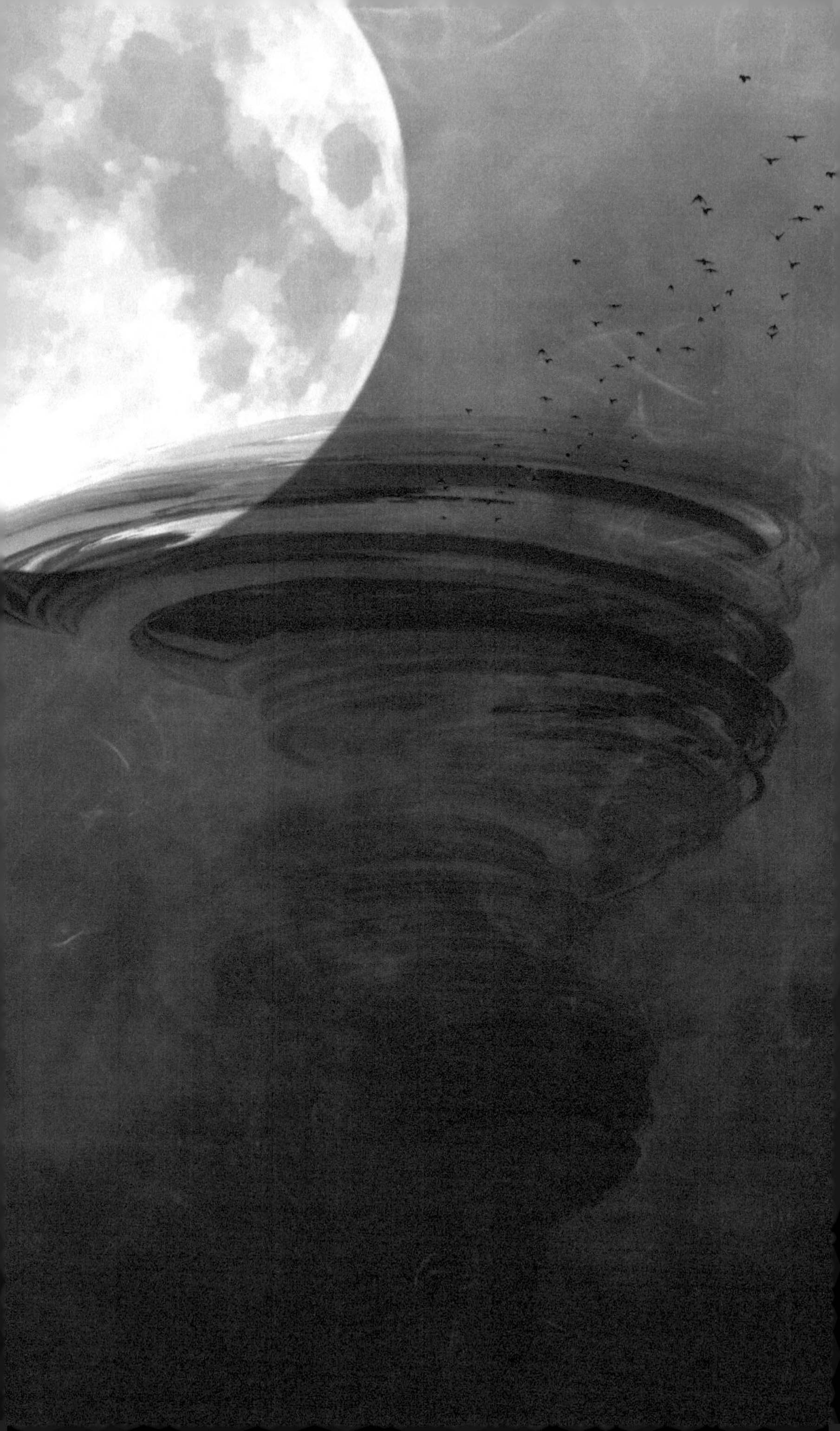

Ten

KES

100 Years Old

"**U**ncle, you must realize how ridiculous you sound by now." Here we are once again with my idiotic uncle attempting to make me his heir. "You just sound desperate at this point. Really, it's not a good look for the King of the Night Court."

For just over seventy years this old bat has been trying to convince me to be his heir in all the wrong ways, and lately it has taken on a mania born out of his slow decay. When fae start to age, it goes quickly. You have a few hundred years at best after you see the first signs. To say my uncle is not handling it well would be an understatement.

"You will capitulate to me—I am your king!" he roars at me. I do not know how to make it any clearer to him that he has no control over me. With aging, his power is slowly leaving him as well. I imagine if it were a fight between our powers, I would win.

I have noticed a connection between the fae he kills and the strength of his power. Each execution gives him a little bump. I am not sure how he does it, or if it's just a gift from the land. Although, I do not think he's gifted by the land at all. I have never seen any great display of power from him in my entire life.

"Hmmm, no, I think not. Imagine if you spent all of this energy attempting to convince the true heir to come back, instead of bending me to your will. I will let you in on a little secret, Uncle—no one bends me to their will. I am a free-spirited bird, and I flit around as I see fit, how I see fit, and where I see fit. Your attempt to build contempt for my cousin has been mediocre at best." I casually lean against a post supporting the circular opening in the roof across from the king.

It was my most recent upgrade to the training facility I spend most of my nights in. It has opened opportunities to train in-flight combat, while using my magic at the same time. Having the freedom to take flight whenever I feel is an added bonus. Flying has become my favorite pastime. The only thing I hear is the sound of wind while I speed through the sky. It clears my head and stretches my wings.

I have even located a perch I particularly enjoy near the border and find myself there regularly.

"He killed your parents! How could you not hold a great contempt for him?" The audacity he has to place the blame for his actions or his will on everyone else except for himself is astounding.

"No, Uncle, *you* killed my parents. It may have been by his hand, however, I know it was not by his will." I shock even myself with the deadly-serious tone I used. My entire body stills the second my parents passed through his mad mouth.

"How dare you place the blame on me!" He truly is quite delusional. I tisk at him and slowly shake my head from side to side as if scolding a youngling. "I am determined to beat the disrespect out of you if it's the last thing I do!" he raged.

"Uncle, the twenty three have not been able to beat me into submission, and at this point I do not think they are even capable of actually beating me," I say with a cocksure grin.

"Perhaps not the twenty three alone; with the help of twenty more warriors, we shall see." At his words, forty three warriors step out from the shadows. He's still doing that. The several warriors who have become my personal trainers, and the closest thing to friends I have, hang back a bit. They know what I have become, because they helped make me.

"Oh, Uncle. My silly, little old uncle, I will warn you now—if you follow through with your threat, there will only be nine still standing by the end of it." His blue face turned nearly black with rage. It has become a fun game for me to come up with new and insulting names for him.

"Ha! You talk a big game, Kestrel." Whenever he uses my full name, I have to fight not to give a reaction. I must not be doing a great job of it since he continues to use it more and more. "For someone who is about to get their plumage taken down a notch." I laugh. At least his bird references have gotten better.

"It's up to you, Uncle, if we play this out and see who comes out right in the end." The murmured warnings from the nine who know me well fall on deaf ears as my uncle raises his hand and snaps his fingers. It's always something. Perhaps theatrics run in the family.

The thirty three warriors, who are all entirely unprepared, fall in around me. The other nine hang back as far as they can without disobeying my uncle. I contemplate if I should make a show of it; make my uncle think he's about to get what he wants before crushing his hopes and dreams. No, better to make a strong show of force.

"Do not say I did not warn you, Uncle. Last chance," I say to the fae circling me. "You can choose to walk away and keep your life, or you can be a forgotten stain on the floor of this blood-soaked arena." Most of them give me a disbelieving smile. They undoubtedly think I am bluffing—I am not. A few of the newcomers look to my uncle and then back to me, deeming me the lesser of the two threats. Their mistake.

The mob continues encroaching as I make a show of stretching and hopping from taloned foot to taloned foot. I let them get close enough to reach out, just a hair shy of getting to me, before I begin my attack.

I grab at the air with my left hand and shoot my fist skyward, stealing all the air from the thirty three I promised death. Most stop in their tracks and panic while a fraction charge at me. This is my favorite trick of all. I let the joy take over my face before I initiate my spin, and my nine companions hit the floor. I spin faster and faster while pulling the cyclone in close. Bringing one arm across my waist and the other across my forehead, I cause the cyclone to compress between my arms until it's nothing but a thin blade of air.

I stop spinning and throw my arms out wide, releasing the cyclone and sending it flying into the crowd around me. When the blade of air meets any being in its path, it easily parts flesh and bone, leaving a macabre circle of torsos and legs. The king, having plenty of warning, ducks just in time. How unfortunate.

"I did warn you, Uncle, and my warning was more for the lives of the fae you just condemned to death. It's a clever little trick I have created, do you not think?" He stares at me with a slack jaw. "It was rather thrilling using it on live creatures for the first time. An unfortunate loss of Night Court warriors, but fun for me all the same." It's a joy watching the king rendered speechless while he stares at the results of his stupidity before letting out a long, defeated sigh. I have never heard anything as wonderful as that sound.

"Fine," he gritted through his teeth. "You win... for now." He stares me down attempting to remain superior, even in the face of failure. "However, you will be a contributing member of this court. I have been receiving reports of Day fae flooding our borders and crossing into the Night Court. It started in the south, so they set up a patrol, and now the Day filth makes their way to the northern border. You and these remaining warriors will patrol the border and do away with any who dare cross into our lands." Well, that was not what I expected him to say.

If this is meant to be some form of punishment, he missed the mark. The idea of hunting the silly, sunny creatures idiotic enough to cross into the darkness makes me feel all tingly inside. This is something I am happy to do. I almost thank him for the assignment—almost.

I have become incredibly bored over the past couple of decades; all I do is train, fly, and fuck whatever fae throws themselves at me. This is going to be great fun. A list of creative ways to play with my prey forms in my mind. I look over to the remaining nine and see them all wearing grins that match my own before returning to look at my uncle.

"Gladly," I say with a wink.

Eleven

CIARAN

123 Years Old

It took me decades to locate the last being in possession of the ring before it fell into my father's manipulative hands. My youngling mind never considered where it came from or questioned such things. Now, I am older and know there is no way my father possesses the vision it requires to make something this convoluted and powerful. This being I have been following all day confirms it.

I have never spent this much time in the Day Court; it's far too bright. I have vague memories of attending the now Day Queen's either mating ceremony or coronation. I was very young, yet I do remember hiding in the few shadows I could find in the Daybreak Palace. There were not many then and there are not many now. I have been creating most of the shadows I need to shield me from view.

I remember, before I was the embodiment of my father's will, I was playful with my shadows, keeping a trail of writhing shadows that followed me everywhere. Once the ring was removed from my body, I felt my shadows looming just within me, but for some reason I could not summon them—or would not.

Not a thought I wish to dwell on.

The trader from many years ago led me to another trader, who led me to a faun in the south of the Day Court. She purchased the ring, costing her nearly all she owned, in order to slip it on to the finger of a leprechaun who cheated her family out of all their prized possessions. She hoped the ring would help her get everything back. It was not lost on me how the leprechaun, in a roundabout way, cheated her out of all of hers as well.

It did not go well for the faun. The leprechaun discovered her attempting to sneak into his room while he slept, stole the ring away from her, and left their town immediately after. Apparently, he took most of the wealth of the town with him. The faun gave the information up freely, and I truly considered letting her live. In the end, I could not risk the chance of her speaking of me to any other being. Besides, I never miss an opportunity to kill a Day Fae. I was generous and made her death quick and painless. Well, at least according to *my* standards. The faun would likely disagree—if she could.

It took me years to find the leprechaun. Ulgridge scanned the realm, listening for hints as to where the little trickster could be hiding. I followed each one he heard, with no success. Until one night, whatever he heard made him positive of the leprechaun's location. I found myself in the Day Court once more, even further south than the faun's town.

There was something unsettling lurking in the town he hid in. Everywhere else in the Day Court has an annoyingly bright gleam; this one looked dull in comparison. Like the sun did not claim it as part of its court. I prefer the darkness, of course, yet this darkness felt *wrong* and something unnatural permeated everything. I did not stick around to investigate; Day problems are not my problems.

I enjoyed slicing that little beast to ribbons. I consider myself to be an impossibly wicked male. This leprechaun, however, was not only wicked, he was deranged as well. He reminded me of my father, the way he carried on conversations with a being that did not exist before giving an answer to any of my questions. Killing him was incredibly satisfying.

He spoke in riddles, making his responses difficult to decipher. The only coherent information I gleaned from him was the most important—the ring. I did not care for, nor desire, whatever powerful magic he tried to bribe me with in exchange for his life. Unfortunately, it was the majority of what left his mouth. The male was a known trickster, and a fool, too, if he thought he could dupe me.

He mentioned giving the ring to a high fae priestess for this ridiculous order he followed; it sounded more like a cult. Their master bade she bring the ring to a temple the realm had forgotten thousands of years ago. Ulgridge took great interest in this information; whatever nonsense they were playing at, I was happy it was happening in the Day Court and not mine.

From the priestess, it transferred hands several more times, making its way up north until finally finding its last stop before my father. A council member of the Day Court, easily lured by the power it held, purchased it for a large sum of gold.

Gold that now belongs to me.

A few times throughout the day, the council member came dangerously close to the dark shadows following him, but each time his gaze never settled on where I hid. I'm lucky there are so many other fae around with decent depths of power, making my own not as noticeable. If not watching closely, he appears to be important and always busy, when in reality he does not do much of any-thing—beyond scheme.

When he began anxiously looking around, I feared dis-covery, until he dipped into a dim, secluded room where two other fae waited. For the last several minutes, I have silently observed the three males shamelessly concoct a plan to commit treason. While hunting down the beings who unintentionally played a hand in my enslavement, I noticed a pattern of events which do not speak well for the future of the Day Court, this meeting included.

"She's young and should be easy to manipulate. How have you both not managed to lead her into place and initiate our plan?" asks one of the fae. The other two, including the one I spent the day with, defer to him on most things, marking him as their unofficial leader.

"*You* lost the one object over a hundred years ago that could have saved us all of this time and effort," he seethes to the fae I plan to make my next victim.

"It's not my fault! There was nothing any of us could have done to bend *him* to our wills. The moment his eyes fell upon it, he somehow knew what it was. You cannot say either of you would have fared any better," he says in a whining voice that makes me itch to snatch him away this instant and take him to my hidden play space back in the Night Court. I still use the table I set up near the falls; it's a tradition of a sort at this point. Every being responsible for the ring landing in my father's hand will die upon it.

"Are you truly this daft? If you had not pulled the ring out, just as he passed by, we would not be having this conversation," the leader says as loud as he dared without drawing unwanted attention.

"Truly, Prafrey, I will never understand what you were thinking, revealing the ring in public during the festivities for the queen's mating ceremony," the last fae says with a tone reserved for scolding younglings.

"I cannot explain it any better than I have told you before—it spoke to me. A voice whispered in my mind to make sure the ring was where it should be and was not damaged. At the same time as I did just as *the whispers* suggested, the Night King waltzed by and his eyes immediately locked on it. As soon as the ring was gone, so were *the whispers*," he whines again, while the others look at him with disbelief.

What a careless thing to do. His stupidity cost me years of my life and something else I have not been able to name. I feel as though something else has been taken from me.

What it is, I do not know, and these are not thoughts I enjoy hosting in my mind. His actions will cost him more than the decade under my father's machinations cost me. I start contemplating whether the other two are just as guilty, when a change of subject grabs my attention.

"Speaking of the Night Court, did either of you hear the latest news?" the leader asks.

"About the queen? Y—," the other one starts to respond.

"Yes, she's dead, and I hope he suffers because of it," Prafrey says, laughing like my mother's death is the greatest comedy.

The news sends me reeling. I do not care much of anything for my mother, but I do not hate her either. I have long held the belief she's a victim of my father as well. The sudden tightening in my chest is as unsettling as it is surprising.

Ulgridge must have known.

Thrown off, I barely notice the meeting has come to an abrupt halt after a noise down the hall spooks them. They get up and leave one by one, my prey is last. I could not have set it up better myself.

I send my shadows out to engulf the dimly lit room, plunging it into darkness. I use them to encapsulate us and create a sound barrier to keep any Day fae from hearing his screams. Prafrey's fear pours from him, I can taste it on the air. I do not usually play with my prey until they are secured to my table, but this male deserves to feel as much terror as I can instill in him.

I say his name quietly before speeding to another spot around him. I repeat the action over and over, sending him into a frenzy. He cannot see where he's going when he tries to run from the darkness. He collides with my wall of shadows and quickly switches his direction, bouncing off the black orb around us.

He begins to call for his mother, as a youngling might. I would not know; I do not remember ever calling for my mother.

Now, I never will.

The game now feels tedious, and I grow bored of it. I sneak up behind him and whisper "boo" into his ear, causing a shrill scream to rip out of him. He turns slowly, and I give him an unhurried, extra-wide smile that makes him scream again. I grab him by the throat and moments later, we are at my favorite spot with the sound of rushing water nearby, instantly soothing my nerves.

Watching the minds of my prey sluggishly process where they are and what has happened is always one of my favorite parts of the night. There are always a few beats of silence while the confusion clears and the reality of their situation becomes clear to them. Some are slower than others. It does not surprise me Prafrey falls into the slower category.

I decide to go back for the other two later; they will give me something to do now that my search is coming to an end. They own as much of the blame as Prafrey does, and honestly, I am not ready for this adventure to end. More than anything else, I feel elation as I pull the leather roll out from its place on the shelf beneath the table.

Finally, understanding dawns on him and he attempts to twist out of the binds securing him to the table. He screams nonsense at me—I will gladly take his screams. I examine my collection, which has grown considerably over the years, and pull out my most recent favorite—a knife with a hooked end that enhances my ability to cleanly carve letters into flesh. Someday I will have the same flourish on skin as I do on parchment.

I contemplate what to carve into his chest while tapping on him in thought. Before I can come to a decision, he begins to beg me with his horribly obnoxious voice. Normally I enjoy listening to their pleas as I work, but this male's voice is intolerable and it interrupts my thoughts.

Faster than he can blink, I reach into his mouth, pull out his tongue, and slice it off.

I let the male choke on his own blood for a few wonderful moments as his power began to knit it together. He begins the long process of regrowing the missing appendage. It's a slow and uncomfortable affair, one he will not live long enough to endure.

The whining voice, now muffled, becomes more of a constant moan—far more enjoyable. I laugh at him, and the creature begins to cry, which only makes me laugh harder. I know exactly what I will carve into him. I take the hooked end and start to carve a clean "D" into his chest. It's a fitting choice for him; a reminder he will carry into his next life and a morbid memorial to Dealla, my mother.

I doubt he finds her comical now.

Twelve

KES

184 Years Old

The Day fae stumbles through the woods while continuously looking over his shoulder. He knows how much danger there is on this side of the border. I crack a branch behind him and have to work to hold in my laughter as the male squeals and falls on his face. This is my favorite part about hunting the intruders.

I port several paces in front of the troll and wait for him to get close enough to fully appreciate the production I am about to put on for him. I grab at the air, allowing it to pick up leaves from the forest floor, before swirling it all around me. I casually lean against a tree, and abruptly end the whirlwind, allowing the leaves to gently fall back down. The male stops short and begins to take slow steps backwards, away from me.

"Well, hello there! Do you come here often?" My friendly tone has him halting his retreat. I love watching the confusion cut across their faces. A pleasant Night fae was not something any Day fae expected to encounter. I give him one of my brilliant smiles, and show off my mouth full of pointed teeth. His eyes widened slightly at the sight, whether it's from my smile or the sharp teeth, I had no way of knowing.

It could always be both.

The troll continues to stare at me, slack jawed. I continue to smile right back at him, giving him time to gather his wits. The other fae patrolling the border are quick to snatch the Day fae they find and dispatch them immediately. They have absolutely no style, no flair, and it sounds horrendously boring. While I admit it's rare to meet a Day fae sneaking across our border with any ability to verbally spar, I still give them the chance to entertain me.

"I...umm...that is to say, no, I do not come here often. I wish to not have to come here at all," the troll finally responds. Just in time, too, I was beginning to grow bored.

"Oh? Why is that? Do you not find the Night Court beautiful?" I ask him, sounding hurt.

"What? No. It...it's very lovely," the troll says, letting out a nervous laugh with his words.

Good, he's starting to relax.

"Then why would you not wish to come to my beautiful home?" I try to sound truly baffled.

"There is nowhere else for me to go. My home is...well, my home is gone. None of the northern communities of trolls will take in any of us southern ones. Apparently, their resources are 'too limited,' which is obviously a lie considering we make everything we need ourselves. I think word is traveling of what plagues the south and communities fear it's catching." This is not the first time I have heard of something plaguing the south of the Day Court. Whatever it is does not seem to be a problem for the Night Court, and that is as far as I am willing to look into it.

"So, you thought you would bring this plague to us?" I make myself sound suspicious of the fae, while inside I am having to keep control of the laughter fighting to bubble out of me.

Soon.

"No! Of course not!" he exclaims, taking a step back. His instincts must be telling him to run, and run fast. It amazes me how few I come across who are smart enough to heed the warning their mind screams at them. Sometimes, if I find them close enough to the border, I will give them a head start and if they can reach the border before I reach them, they live to try again.

If they dare.

They are not trying to stay in the Night Court; they are attempting to travel *through* it. There is some rumor of a land out to sea in the west. They are all chasing a lie; there is nothing out there. The tales these Day fae recite were enough to spark a bit of curiosity. I even flew out over the sea from north to south and north again—there is nothing out there.

"Well, if you do not wish to be here, and you cannot stay in the Day Court, why not stay in the Borderlands with the witches?" I love asking this question. They each have a memory of a different encounter with a different coven, and I find them all wildly amusing. I have no love for the witches, however, even I can admit their tactics are inspiring.

"The *witches*," he says, like the word is a curse. "I tried to. I even began to build a little home for myself, but every time I got near enough to finish, those little hea-thens would show up and turn my hard work into any number of nonsensical things. One even made it into a wooden frog!" I almost let the grip on my laughter slip at the murder flaring in the troll's voice over a few little youngling witches. They are admirable troublemakers, I will give them that.

"That seems like a waste of a witch's time. Surely they have more important things to deal with?" The troll throws his hands up in exacerbated agreement.

"The grown witches seem to. It's the little terrors of younglings that need to be taken in hand by their elders. They even giggled while tormenting me! Giggled!" The mischief those youngling witches created is enough to earn my respect.

"Younglings? You mean to tell me you could not handle a few baby witches? That is rather embarrassing for you, if I do say so myself." My laughter finally works its way out, and the troll looks angry for the first time since we initiated our little dance.

"There was a mob of them!" he exclaims, his anger growing further as my laughter increases.

Good.

"You could not handle a few wee witches, but you thought you could handle the entire Night Court? I think I should be insulted, but I can only seem to find the humor in your stupidity," I say through laughter. If the troll was mad before, he's near boiling now.

"I only need to sneak across and find a boat. I am not staying here!" he yells.

"Oh, are you trying to reach the mysterious land across the water?" My question makes him look at me with hope shining in his eyes while the anger slips away.

"You truly are a fool!" I cackle, really making it a production. "No, please—please stop. I cannot breathe." I say while grabbing my knees, placing my head between them, and making a show of attempting to calm down. I stand back up and wipe imaginary tears from my eyes.

"There is no land across the water—I looked myself. Such a fool," I say in between a few more chuckles.

"But...but, there must be," the troll says softly.

"Furthermore, how in the realm did you think you could possibly make it across the entire Night Court? You barely made it past the border before I found you." I lean against the tree again, adopting a careless posture.

"There must be—many of my brethren have crossed your land before me." He sounded so sure of himself, the poor little fella.

"Not a single Day fae has made it across the entirety of the Night Court. Come to think of it, I do not think a single one has made it even halfway across." I find it all too amusing watching him work out what has become of his "brethren." When he looks at me again, the fear is back with a vengeance and he begins to back away.

"You killed them? All of them?" he asks, sounding shocked.

"Not all of them." He looks slightly relieved at that. "After all, I am not the only being patrolling the border. It would be impossible for me to kill all of your kind with the others hanging around." The mild relief instantly vanishes and he turns to run.

I *love* it when they run.

He does not get very far; trolls are incredibly slow. I grab his arm and flip him to the ground before creating pressure with the air around him to hold him down. The troll begins to screech and squirm, making a desperate attempt to escape.

"You did not think you were getting out of this alive, did you?" I ask and squat down next to him. I tisk while I pat him on the face with mock sadness. "I should probably let you know, most of my fellow border patrols give a swift death and move on to the next. I find that to be such a waste. You and I are going to have so much fun! Well," I say thoughtfully looking down at the troll, "at least I will."

I tap the being on the forehead and send him to a table in a private section of the dungeon I claimed for myself several decades ago. I like to give them a few minutes by themselves. They work themselves into quite a frenzy. It's highly entertaining.

I do a full body stretch while breathing in deep the crisp scent of the woods surrounding me. The scent always brings comfort, while also stirring up memories better left alone. I do not have time to think of my cousin, nor do I wish to. Over the years, I have come to terms with the hand he played in the death of my parents.

I have *not*, however, forgiven him for leaving me here to deal with his wretched father. At least he finally gave up trying to force me into being his heir. He has moved on to bribery. It will never work, but he does not need to know that. I gladly take the gifts he sends my way.

Porting to the dungeon, the troll is doing exactly what I hoped he would—screaming. I clap my hands together in excitement, grabbing his attention. His eyes blow wide and he begins to writhe even harder while I walk to the wall of sharp toys displayed.

"Please, just let me go. I will never cross the border again," he says with a shrill voice.

"You certainly will not be crossing the border again, and I am sorry to break it to you, I am fresh out of free passes."

Only *once* have I ever let a Day fae go.

I walk past the pointy, sharp things before coming to my favorite part of the display, the bludgeons. I grab the smallest one; I like to start slowly and build up to the finale. I am never one to pass up a chance to create a spectacle out of a Day fae.

You have before.

I had followed the nymph, just as I did the troll, somehow not seeing what she carried with her. When I made my big reveal, she immediately turned to run. One of the few smarter Day fae I have come across. I cornered her again a few moments later and that was when I saw it. She carried a very small youngling across her chest—a small boy.

I still remember how the smile fell from my face when the female pleaded not for her own life, but for that of her child's. It was impossible not to compare her to my own mother, and it was for that reason, and that reason alone, I escorted her and her son to the edge of the border. I told her if she's found in the Night Court ever again, she will not receive the same kindness. I explained there was no land across the water and demanded she never allow small younglings to cross the border—ever.

Since that day, I have never come across another youngling, and as far as I know, neither had any of my comrades. The same fate the troll is about to meet, would have befallen that nymph. The love she showed for her son was a reminder of the love my mother showed me a long time ago. There will *never* be another Day fae left alive if caught on our side of the border. No troll, and definitely no nymph.

Thirteen

CIARAN

263 Years Old

The clash of swords is amplified by the echoes the cave creates. When Ulgridge had me practice defending myself against him for the first time, I was surprised the sword survived the first strike it blocked. The final of the three scheming fae responsible for allowing the ring to come into my father's orbit happened to be a collector of magical items—this sword being one of them.

"Your feet," he says, never giving me a long winded correction, which I appreciate. Neither of us desire conversation. Every so often he tells me some tale he has created, speaking more words to me within one story than he does in between each one. I spoke even less.

I used to listen to his stories, intrigued by the worlds he created, but as the years have passed I tune him out more often than not. I prefer to stay in my own mind, thinking over my return to Nightfell. I will make sure my father is as much a prisoner in his own body as he made me in mine. The ring may no longer work the same way, but I can make it so he never moves again.

"Moon Blessed," his gravelly voice declared as he came down hard with his hulking sword, pulling me from my own thoughts.

"What?" I ask, sure I have missed something.

"Moon Blessed," he says again, as if I should know what he's talking about. "Your sword and the ring. The metal is Moon Blessed."

"There is a 'moon blessed' metal? Where would I find this metal?" He laughs at the skepticism in my voice, causing me to drop my guard. I dodge his sword. Even with my speed, I narrowly missed a few nights of healing.

"No, it's normal metal that is Moon Blessed. It has been a long time since the power of moonlight existed. Fae with the power can use it to create anything desired out of any metal and transform it into something Moon Blessed." While he speaks, I attack, hoping to catch him off guard. He easily blocks me. In all these years I have never been able to catch him unaware, no matter how quiet or how quick I am.

"There is no such thing as 'moonlight' power." I am certain of it. "I have never once come across any mention of such a power." I have been raiding the libraries scattered across the Night Court for a couple hundred years searching for a way to break the curse the witch placed upon my line generations ago. I will find a way, and I will be the true king with all the power of the land I am owed.

"I have no doubts, not with the purge your ancestor dictated centuries ago. He embarrassed himself and decided it would be better to delete the history of the Night Court, starting with his blunder, than have a record of his actions," he says while shaking his head in disgust. If that is true, how much history am I missing and how old is Master Ulgridge?

"Such a shame. Many of the most important events that have shaped this realm, and some of the most incredible things to be made in the Night Court, were all purged. A loss of unimaginable proportions for the realm." The more he says, the more I believe him.

"A rather convenient excuse if you ask me, leaving no proof of this 'moonlight' power you claim exists." He comes at me harder and faster, causing me to shift my attention to the sword coming at me in quick succession.

"Warriors in head to toe Moon Blessed armor went into battle next to their counterparts in golden Sun Blessed armor. They were light and flexible, and also held strong spells within them." It's my turn to laugh.

"Now, I know you are making this up. You mean to tell me, not only did both courts fight side by side—I am assuming Sun Blessed is the balance to Moon Blessed—but also witches willingly placed spells upon them? You expect me to believe that?" He shrugs, then switches up his technique.

"It does not matter to me. You can believe me or not. If you wish to be an ignorant fool, that is your prerogative," he says with a grin. He knows that will ignite my rage, and it works. I switch to offense, forcing him to defend against me; using my anger is a common trick he uses to switch sides during practice.

"I am no fool!" I seethe. "Why would I believe such fantasy from a male hiding in the mountains who is known to tell fairy tales?" He looks me in the eyes while never missing a single one of my strikes, and cocks his head to the side.

"I am not the only male hiding in the mountains, and I have never told a single fairy tale." I scoff at his words.

"Again, it makes no difference to me if you choose to be a fool."

"If what you say is true, what was so important to bring both courts and the witches together?" I ask with a smirk, seeing how far he's willing to take this tall tale of his.

"The fate of the realm," is all he responds.

"And what was so threatening to the fate of the realm to make the impossible possible?" Never, in all of time, would the Night and Day Courts come together and fight side by side.

"Maybe impossible now—it was not always. Why should I tell you? You are convinced this is nothing but a fantasy," he sounds...is he disappointed? He drops his sword and steps back.

"Enough for today. There is one last thing to tell you. I am hearing mutterings about your father." My eyes shoot to meet his. "Ah, I see in this you will choose to believe my words."

"What have you heard?" I ask, barely able to get a breath in.

"Your father has aged faster than any king before him. He's now confined to his bed." I feel my entire body sag, an invisible weight I have been carrying around with me immediately dissipates. I throw my head back and roar with laughter. My father, in his lifelong quest for power, thought he would live forever. Now, not only is he bedridden, but also powerless. This, I have to see.

The entire confrontation I spent most of my life preparing for is no longer an option. I always assumed he would still be full of vitality, not an invalid, when we reunited. Now, I no longer know what I will say. Maybe it's better this way; it will be my true thoughts pouring from my mouth.

I wonder if anyone will recognize me, which is stupid because I look so much like my father. I will never be able to forget him, not with my face being a constant reminder. This does not upset me, because I remember thinking how terrifying my father looked to me as a small youngling, and it pleases me to be just as terrifying—maybe even more so.

I cannot wait to see the look on my father's face when he sees me for the first time. I hope he fears my wrath. Fears a death at my hands. Part of me has always desired to kill him and be done with it. The other, larger part of me wants to see him suffer the way I did. It's disappointing, knowing I will be unable to bring him to the same level of suffering with the ring as it is now. It does not matter—he *will* suffer.

I will make sure of it.

I look to Ulgridge for the first time since he gave me the news. He grins and nods a farewell, knowing what I am about to say.

"It's time to go home."

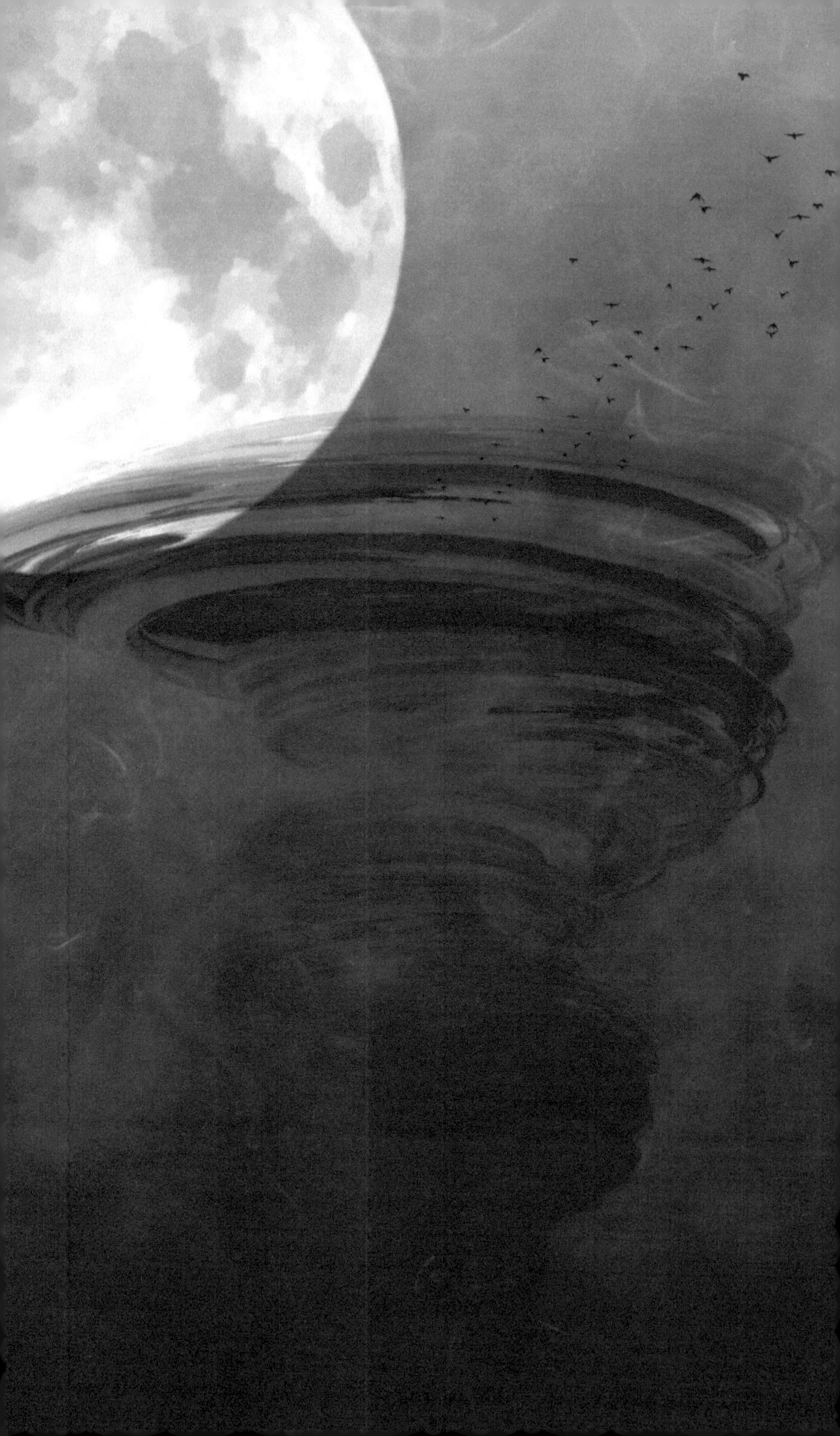

Fourteen

KES

The Return

The past several nights have been the best of my life. My uncle has been confined to his bed, too weak to stand, which means every time he calls on me, I can ignore him. The constant parchment in my face is becoming obnoxious, but not enough for me to heed his summons. I do not even give him the satisfaction of a reply.

After I visit one of my female acquaintances—she does this thing with her snake-like tongue that I swear makes me see the gods—I will go hunting along the border. Lately, the border crossings have been few and far between, which I find incredibly boring. I love flying across the night sky, however, I am itching to practice the precise, detailed work I have been trying to perfect with my air magic.

It's one of my more gruesome inventions. I am able to force the thinnest blades of air widthwise through the body and keep them alive until I am ready to expand the sheets to create an interesting view of the captured Day fae's body. It reminds me of looking through a window. Sometimes you can even watch the heart make its last couple beats. Now, I am trying to perfect doing the same thing lengthwise. It's much harder than I thought it would be.

I port outside the door to…I honestly cannot remember her name. I have been calling her "The Tongue" in my head, and something tells me she would not be happy if I called her that to her face. Lish…Lish-something…it's something like that. I am about to knock on her door when I overhear a conversation down the hall.

"Have you heard?" a female voice asks.

"That the prince is back?" another female voice asks.

"Yes!" the first one says with a squeal of excitement. "I saw him just a few moments ago—he's so terrifying! It took every ounce of willpower to not immediately throw myself at him. He's wicked, with a capital 'Wick'!" I have no idea what that means, though they seem to based on their uncontrollable laughter.

"It's going to be so nice having some fresh meat in the palace," the second one says.

"Oh, I think it will be more than 'nice.'" Another round of giggles.

"Do not mistake me, Kes is..." the first one starts, "delicious."

"An experience," the other one says. I puff my chest out and know I am grinning. "Delicious" and an "experience," they said. My male ego grows tenfold.

"But," the first one says slowly.

There's a "but?"

"I have had him *many* times. He never disappoints, however, Ciaran is unknown. That sounds thrilling." They both release a sigh simultaneously before breaking into giggles again as they walk arm in arm further down the hall. Ciaran is back and already he's disturbing my life.

Ciaran is back.

Of course he's back. I bet he came running the second he heard his father was now a sack of potatoes. He will claim the throne and the eyes of every female in Nightfell palace. I am not sure which annoys me most.

I have enjoyed having the throne thrust at me, only to continuously reject it and the king. I have half a mind to claim it first just to make his life difficult. It's the least he deserves for leaving me the focus of his father's attention. Reluctantly, I can admit, it has worked out well for me in the end. I cannot be sure I would be as skilled as I am now. Besides, what does not kill you makes you more dramatic, and I do love to be dramatic.

No longer feeling like seeing "The Tongue," and feeling like a moron for standing in front of her door for this long, I port to my training facility. It does belong to me; I have claimed it with the blood I have spilled, marking it as mine. Even though nearly a hundred years have passed since my blood soaked this floor, I earned this part of the palace.

It has been just as long since I had a sparring partner of even caliber. The warriors, who once tormented me and then trained me, spend most of their time hunting the border and moving from one city or town to another looking for trouble. It does not matter, I outgrew them many decades ago.

Maybe Ciaran will be an even match.

I do not know how he could be; who knows where he has been all of the years. How could he have trained anywhere of note without his father hearing of it? It's likely he will be no match for me, though I would love to find out. If I beat his ass in the process, even better. I could put on quite the production and show the entire court I could be king if I desired it. Being king still sounds like the worst form of torture—perfect for my cousin.

I contemplate the many ways I can humiliate my cousin as I go through my poses, incorporating my air magic into each one. It has become second nature to move in tandem with it; I no longer need to think or concentrate anymore. It just comes to me because it's me. We are one in the same.

After several hours, I am still harboring a wild sort of energy inside me and take to the skies to rid myself of it. Second night came at some point during my workout, leaving the crescent moon high in the sky. This is my favorite time of night. The darkness is richer with a thicker feel to the air, creating the perfect camouflage. It's unfortunate for someone who only wants to stand out, though it is beautiful. Almost as beautiful as me.

Ha!

The night air is calming as the current of air I create while flying caresses me. This is the one place I can drop the shield I have built around myself. Although, each year the shield melts further into me, stealing more of the Kes I once was. I wonder how long it will be until the shield and I are one—another hundred years? I wish it would happen sooner. There is no place for the old Kes anywhere in the Night Court, and I am ready to banish him forever. Let the shield harden around my heart, leaving no space for another to occupy it.

I land back in the training facility. Removing the roof so many years ago was the best choice I ever made. I feel refreshed, and apparently hungry, as my stomach loudly informs me. I port to my chambers, snap my fingers, and a meal appears on the large table in the lounge.

I still only port into the lounge of my chambers, never my room, the office, or the other room that was once *theirs*. I finally rid myself of their things several decades ago and made the chambers my own. The second room has remained empty, while I try to figure out what to do with it. I do not need another study or a place to train; my own room is large enough to easily contain all I own. I have no use for it, and if it's going to be useless, it might as well look as though it serves a purpose. I will make it a guest room at some point, for the guests I will never have.

Just as I sit down to eat, a spelled parchment appears in front of my face. This one is not from the king. It has been a long time, but I would recognize that penmanship any-where, even if it no longer has the sloppiness of a youngling attached to it. I laugh at the request and send no reply.

And so it begins.

FIFTEEN

CIARAN

The Prince of Darkness

I port to the great hall where the most beings are likely to be, making as big of an entrance as possible. The second I arrive, I start the walk to my father's chambers. I could port there, but I want as many Night fae to see I have returned, making gossip spread faster. I am not one for dramatics, unless it serves a purpose, like the spectacle I am currently creating.

I walk with my wings slightly spread. I send my shadows out to fill up every place I occupy with each step I take, giving the illusion of being darkness itself. It does not take more than a few minutes for the name "Prince of Darkness" to be whispered.

Prince of Darkness—I like it.

By the time I reach the entrance to my father's chambers, I am certain the entire palace is aware I have returned and word has likely already begun spreading to the city. I do not bother knocking and let myself in. The room smells of decay and mold with a dampness permeating it, fitting for a being like him.

I hear nothing, and for a moment I fear I am too late and will never get to say everything I spent decades preparing. I move with the unnatural speed I have become accustomed to and silently enter his bedchambers. Without thought, my shadows fill the room, darkening it even further.

"I knew you would come back," says a watery voice from somewhere beneath the pile of blankets in the center of the overly large four post bed. I say nothing. I find if I remain silent others feel the need to fill it and often make themselves sound like a fool. I know my father will not be able to stop himself; he has always been a fan of his own voice. I hope he cringes every time he hears how weak he sounds.

"I tried to make that useless cousin of yours accept becoming my heir, just so I could take it away when you finally showed your face again," he says, sounding like the fool I knew he would. He said he "tried," meaning Kes never accepted, and the only reason he did was to play some childish prank on him.

A fool, indeed.

I continue to remain silent until he becomes uncomfortable enough with it. I can hear him struggling to sit up. The urge to laugh is almost impossible to ignore, but my desire to intimidate him with silence wins out. When he finally emerges from his cocoon of blankets, the male I see has a paperiness to him. A soft breeze could blow him away, like ash in the wind. His body finally matches his mind—weak.

"Speak when you are spoken to boy! I am the king!" he rages. He sounds like a youngling throwing a fit, and I can no longer hold in my laughter.

"And what a poor excuse for a king you are. Look at you, nothing beyond a rotting corpse, slowly returning to the realm. Is that what your insatiable appetite for power was meant to circumvent? Only for it to come for you sooner than any king in history. At least you will be known for something, although it's not something I would wish to be remembered for," I say with one of my wide smirks.

"And what will *you* be remembered for? The prince who ran away? The prince who feared his father?" He lets out a dry laugh that sounds more like a gasp than amusement.

"Ah. Well you see, *Father*, I have been very busy." I say nothing more, waiting for his curiosity to get the better of him.

"And what kept you so busy you thought you could deny your duties as my son?" His voice is losing the minimal power behind it with each word he speaks.

"What were these duties you speak of? Being a constant source of power you could feed from?" I let out an amused chuckle. "That is a duty I would deny no matter the circumstance." He mumbles something about "ungrateful younglings" in response.

"As for what kept me so busy, I spent a lot of time hunting. I visited every library in the Night Court, and even a few in the Day Court, looking for any mention of the curse you told me of while on one of your power-drunk rants." He perks up a bit, and shockingly, it looks like hope trickles into his milky eyes. He cannot possibly think I have come to save him from the curse. What a fool. I will take great pleasure in watching his hope dissolve.

"Unfortunately, in all my searching, I have not found any mention of the curse you spoke of. The only reason I even believe you is because when I attempt to speak of it to anyone else, my lips are unable to form the words." It did not seem possible for him to sag any further into himself, yet at my, words he does.

"Oh, Father, I do hope you were not entertaining the idea I could possibly be here to save you. Even if I learned how to break it, why would I ever help you?" I smile, watching the rage take over him.

"Because, I am your father!" he tries to yell, but it sounds more like a loud whisper than anything else.

"Some father you have been, enslaving your only son in his own body through trickery and cursed bits of metal." It was an effort not to allow my own rage to show, when a smirk, not so unlike my own, crossed his face.

"Speaking of," I reach into my pocket and reveal the ring I have carried with me all of these years, waiting for this exact moment. My father's face pales to a near grayish tone. "I was busy hunting for something else, alongside information about the curse. I located each and every being responsible for allowing this ring to find its way into your possession. This bit of metal has been on a rather entertaining adventure. I enjoyed hearing how the ring changed hands, over and over, before I killed them, slowly. There is only one being left responsible for this ring ending its journey on my finger."

"You have come to kill me then, have you? You waited until it was mostly done for you, like a coward. Were you afraid you would not be able to kill me before?" he asks with no small amount of disgust in his voice. "Get on with it then, boy."

"Why would I kill you?" He looks at me with confusion. "When there are far worse things than death." Finally, my father's face fills with fear.

"You will not kill me?" The way my father asks makes me realize that is exactly what he hopes I am here to do.

"No, as you said, it's 'mostly done' already." The look of dismay he wears is a sight I will not soon forget.

"Originally, my plan was to place this ring on your finger and make you frozen in one position for the rest of your existence, with no one for company besides the voice in your head. Where is it now? Has your own insanity abandoned you along with your health?" He glares at me.

"He left me years ago when my decline began to increase, I could be of no more assistance to his cause," somehow he says this as if he completely understands and even supports the voice's departure. Gods, I hope I never inherit the same illness of the mind.

"So here you lie, a prisoner in your own body, without so much as the voice in your head to keep you company. It appears fate has already gifted me what I desire most. No, Father, I will not kill you. I am going to leave you here...to rot...alone." With that, I turn on my heels and walk out of his bedchambers, while he begs and pleads to my back for me to end him.

I have never felt such overwhelming joy in my entire life. I walk slowly out of his chambers, listening to his weak cries the whole way to the door. The sound of him begging me for death is one I have craved to hear for over two hundred years. Amazingly, it required nothing for me to hear them, except turn my back to him. Stepping out, I shut the door on my father, along with the part of my life I allowed him to control for so long. Years ago, when I escaped the palace and Ulgridge removed my hand, I thought I was free.

Now, I *know*, I am free.

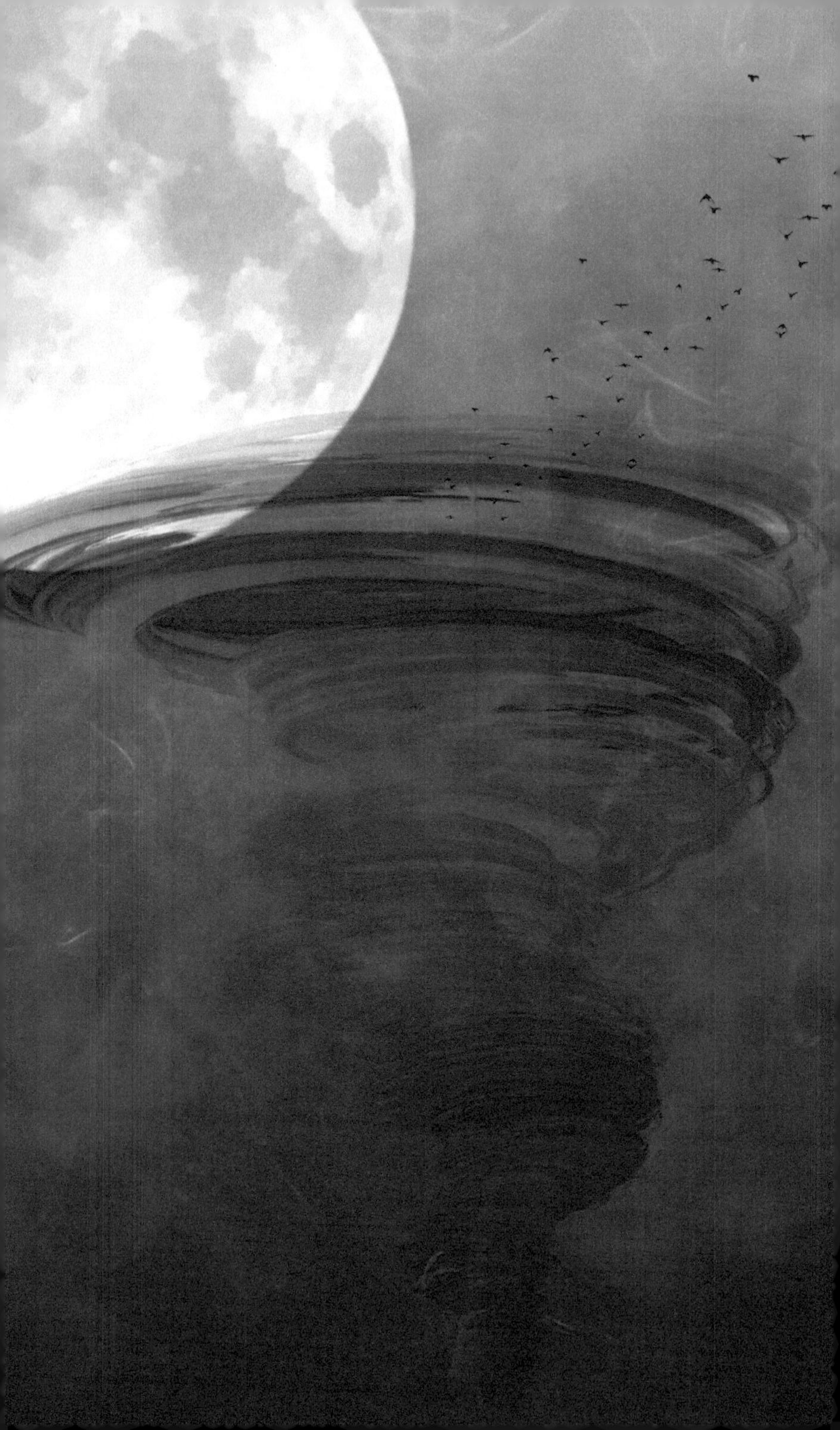

Sixteen

KES

The Art of Distraction

I contemplated not coming, but curiosity got the better of me. Plus, this meeting gives me an excellent opportunity to annoy the shit out of my cousin. I did not think it possible, yet he has even less of a personality now than he did when we were younglings. Even the way he sits in his chair is rigid and bland; he has absolutely no flair.

I stroll into the meeting much later than the requested time. After all, fae do not follow any rigid time structure. We arrive when we arrive. Color me surprised when I entered and found Ciaran not here. I thought for sure I would be the last to show. Not even two minutes after I choose a seat to throw my body across, he strides in.

You cannot port into the council chamber, thanks to some spell placed on the room long ago by magic unknown to any Night fae in existence tonight. I love the drama; it's the perfect opportunity to make a grand en-trance—a lost art to the fae who port. I was hoping to cause a disruption, maybe cut him off mid sentence and have dramatically brooding battle of glares. I had it all planned in my head. Typical Ciaran, ruining everything for me.

He makes his way to the other side of the room, chooses a seat, and turns it into a less ostentatious throne. I would have gone for the most extravagant and horrifically gaudy thing I could imagine, and my imagination is rather im-pressive. He had yet to take even the smallest glance in my direction.

Irritating.

The second he takes his seat and opens his mouth to speak, I summon an unopened bottle of wine, a glass I make sure to rattle against the bottle, and a bottle opener I have no idea how to use. I always use my power or my mag-ic to remove the stopper wedged into the neck of a bottle. This should be fun to figure out, but more importantly, it will be distracting. I already have laughter trying to work its way out of me just thinking about the annoyance on my cousin's face.

He pauses for one solitary moment before moving on to whatever he has planned to say, without acknowledging my distraction. Frustrated with my inability to crack his cool indifference, I make a huge production of trying to remove the stopper, making more noise than necessary. He does not so much as trip over his words before shadows wrap their way around the bottle and my hands, silencing my efforts.

I barely pay attention to any of the words he says. Something about his father no longer being fit to rule and he will take his place as *the* prince of the Night Court. He says it like there is not another prince sitting across from him. With the exception of the shadows leaving my hands, he *still* does not acknowledge my existence.

Very irritating.

I can be just as distracting without making much noise. I get up slowly, making sure my chair scrapes across the floor in the process. This feels like the perfect time to make my way around the room and admire the art displayed on the walls as Ciaran keeps speaking. In all honesty, using the term "art" to describe any of these pieces is a stretch. The council members glance back and forth between us, uncertain who to give their attention.

I can not tell you who a single fae sitting around this table is, with the exception of my cousin and Balric. Somehow the annoying cunt wound up on the council, and he looks less than pleased to see either of us at the table now.

I can practically hear the wheels spinning in his head as he begins some plot against either one or both of us.

It takes me a moment to notice the room is silent, and I can feel eyes on me. I was lost in the less than stellar descriptive words circulating through my mind about the image in front of me. I take my time, knowing they are all waiting on me, inspecting every square inch of the painting I can only guess is meant to depict the hunt. It really is atrocious, and not in a delightful way. I am surprised my eyes have not started to bleed.

"Have any of you looked at this painting before?" I ask, sounding truly curious and not like I am trying to waste more time.

"I painted it myself—for the king," Balric says proudly.

"Ah, that explains it. It's truly the worst thing I have ever laid my eyes on, and that is really saying something. Congratulations on being woefully lacking again," I say, turning to look at him with fake enthusiasm. I will never grow tired of seeing that ugly face fall into indignant rage. Out of the corner of my eye I see Ciaran's mouth quirk up the slightest bit in amusement.

He might have a personality greater than a rock after all.

"The king loved it so much he had it framed and hung it himself on that very wall," Balric brags with an overinflated arrogance he has no right to contain.

"Well, I think it's safe to say the king has horrible taste." I give him one of my brilliant smiles and add a wink for good measure. There is a collective gasp from the council members around the table.

"How dare you speak of your king in such a way!" the goblin admonishes. My gods, how did I not notice *that* face? The creature hit every branch on his way down the ugly tree. The way his face jiggles while he yells is enough to send me over the edge into a fit of laughter.

"My father is nothing more than a pile of rotting dust hiding beneath a fortress of blankets, and he has always been an imbecile. As are each of you if you never noticed his insanity. Did you ever observe him having arguments with the voices in his head?" Ciaran asks in a tone that speaks volumes on what he thinks of the beings around the table.

"Ha! Yes, I called it his 'invisible friend' and asked him to indicate where it stood while I was *blessed* by his presence. I found it hilarious, he did not, which made it all the more amusing." Ciaran let out a single bark of laughter.

This might not be as bad as I thought.

All of the council members look at us as though we are the crazy ones. I return to my seat and wait for whatever it was I missed to be repeated. I lounge across the seat and create some wind to blow my feathers around; the females tell me it makes me look "regal." Ciaran does not open his mouth to repeat himself, and I do not open mine to ask what was said, creating a heavy silence that makes the other beings shift uncomfortably in their seats.

"Prince Ciaran said you are to be his General, as is the custom for a second prince," the lone female says, unable to bear the silence any longer. I make a noise that is no more an acceptance than it is a dismissal.

"He's untrained!" Balric bellows, thinking he knows everything, as usual. "He has not been trained in the art of strategy or with a sword. I never once saw him in the training yard for instruction." For someone who prides himself on having his nose in everyone's business, he sure missed the mark on this one. I always assumed it was common knowledge that I have been hunting the border for the last two hundred and some odd years.

How many think the same? This needs to be rectified. I must find a way to make a huge production that will allow me to show off just how skilled I am. I cannot allow the females of the palace the opportunity to not admire all of my skills, in and out of the bedchambers. I look at my cousin and consider the plan I concocted yesternight. He does not have the air of someone who is untrained, which makes me desire going up against him even more.

Could he actually be a worthy opponent?

"I will gladly be your general," Balric says while puffing his slender chest out. Can *he* even hold a sword? He looks like he's still in an awkward youngling growth phase, or perpetually stuck in one. The thought makes me chuckle and he glares at me, making me laugh even more.

"Oh, you sweet little Balric. I thought you knew everything that transpires within the walls of the palace," I say with mock confusion.

"I do," he responds, a little less certain than before.

"No, I think not." The way he shakes with fury makes my heart leap with joy. "If you did, you would know the king took it upon himself to educate me in a very," I pause searching for the right word, "*inventive* way. His methods, while interesting, were effective. Who did you think was patrolling the border all of these years?" The confusion on his face makes me laugh again.

"Do not tell me you knew nothing of the Day fae flooding our lands." I can see his mind searching through every little thing he has tucked inside it and coming up empty.

"It's alright, Balric. Try not to beat yourself up too much. On second thought, please do. It would be hilarious to watch."

"As entertaining as this has been to observe, what I am hearing, Kes, is you are more than capable of being my general. Wonderful—this meeting is dismissed." Ciaran gets up and casually strolls towards the door, taking his shadowy darkness with him. I throw a gust of wind and send them scattering. He pauses. Our eyes lock for the first time in centuries and hold for a few breaths before he reforms his shadows and exits the room.

I am going to kick his blue, prickly ass.

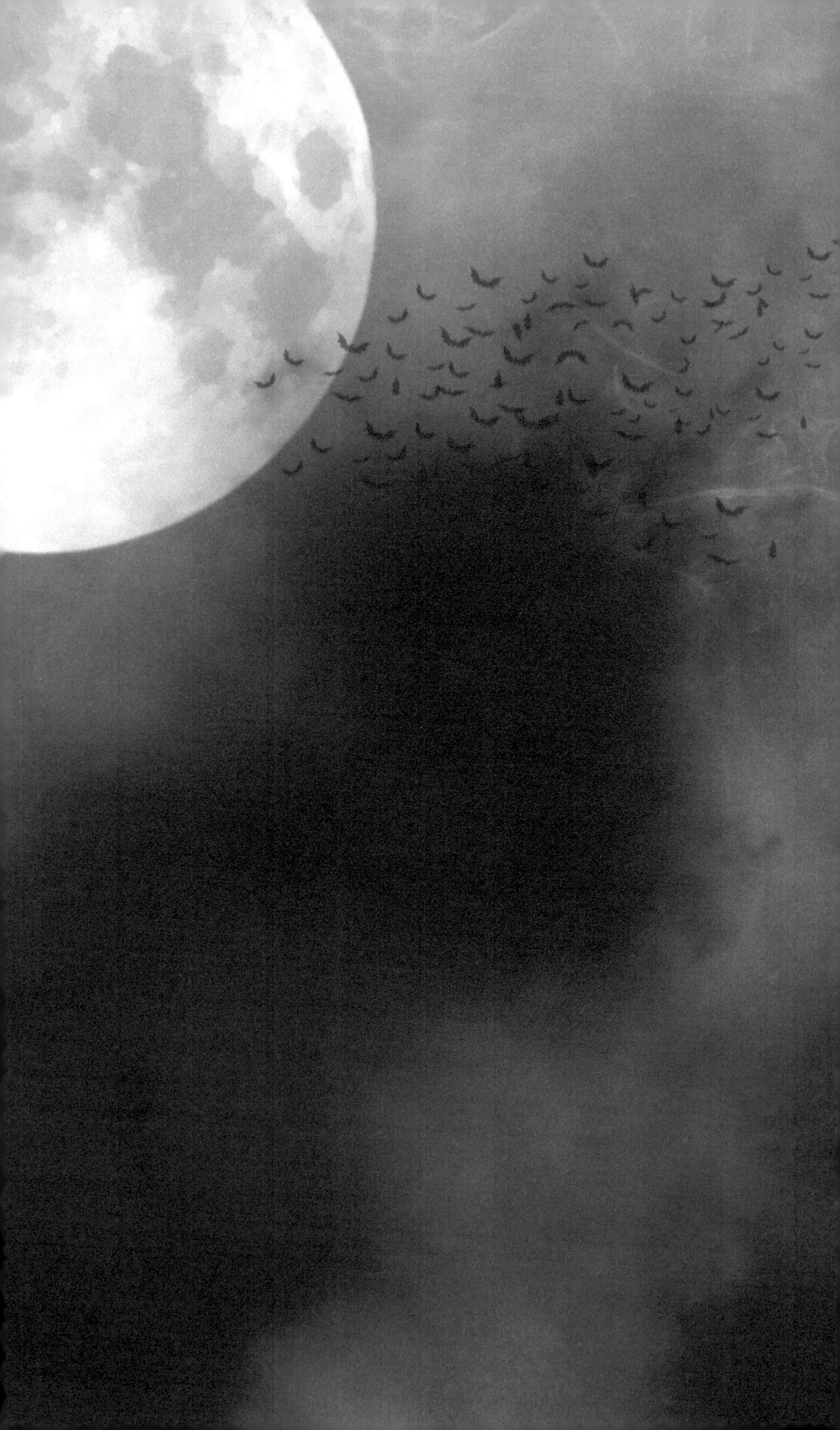

Seventeen

Ciaran

Challenge Accepted

Kes is obnoxious and yet oddly entertaining, when his antics are not directed at me. Anytime our paths cross he uses that stupid wind of his to swirl my shadows around. It's annoying, yet it has taught me to strengthen my control over them. Sometimes, he sends a cyclone and I wrap my shadows around it making his cyclone look like a swirling mass of darkness before I am able to snuff it out entirely. Each time he laughs like it's his favorite game in the realm. I actually think it truly might be.

It has been months since I returned, and it's the same thing every time—I grow tired of it. Every single thing he does is a spectacle, which is annoying in and of itself; however, even more so is the way he constantly tries to push his theatrics more and more each time. It's as though he competes with his past self to see who is more dramatic. Which is exactly what he's currently doing.

I loathe these meetings. The creatures surrounding the table are all idiots, with the possible exception of Kes. He may seem to not pay attention, creating some distraction or another, yet he's quick to make any of the other council members the laughing end of a joke. He makes them feel like the idiots they are each time they are wrong, while also telling them, in a melodramatic way, the obvious response. *That* is always entertaining—*this* is not.

Kes has been faux lamenting the death of my father, loudly, for the last half hour or so. It was funny for a total of two seconds, before it became annoying. He lets out a loud moan of such obvious mock sadness he has a hard time not laughing, which he promptly tries to pull off as crying.

"Kes!" I yell, and he lets out an even louder wail. I stand and bang on the table making everyone, except him, jump. I do gain his attention though.

"Yes, my father is dead. No, I do not care, and I am guessing this is some kind of celebration for you, albeit a strange one. I do not care if you waste these idiot's time, however, I will not tolerate you wasting mine. Pull yourself together, or get the fuck out of here." He slowly stands and cocks his head to the side, wearing one of those ridiculous fake smiles.

"What are you going to do about it?" he asks as he places his hands on the table and leans towards me. "Oh, mighty blue one." He has been challenging me as often as he can, and I cannot understand what his motivations are.

"Do not test me. I am officially the ruler of the Night Court now—"

"Are you? Says who? What if I want to be king?" He cannot be serious. The rest of the council members' heads volley between each of us, slack jawed, with obvious discomfort. All except Balric, who looks gleeful watching the production Kes has forced me into. It makes me want to rip his head from his shoulders.

"You have never shown interest in the crown. However, if I must, I will remove anyone or anything that tries to stand between me and what is rightfully mine, you feathered fool!" I rage at him. Based upon the huge smile splitting his face—real this time—I feel like I may have reacted the exact way he wanted me to, which irritates me even further, making it two heads I wish to remove.

"Wonderful! Then tomorrow, when the full moon rises for first night, we shall meet on one of the flat plains just north of the palace. We shall see who is to be the rightful heir to the throne," he says with true excitement in his voice. Killing my cousin is not something I desire, but now he leaves me no choice.

Tomorrow, Kes will die.

The full moon comes and I port to the agreed upon location at nearly the same time as Kes. I am surprised to see my cousin in casual, nondescript attire when he usually wears something extravagant and *shiny*. The several fae gathering, eager to watch one of their heirs die, does not surprise me. They circle the plain close enough to have a good view, but not close enough to become collateral damage.

Maybe he will be a worthy opponent.

"Cousin, it's not too late for you to walk away and keep your life intact. I would not allow this concession to any other in your position." I give him this one opportunity out of some misguided feeling of a debt owed to him and his parents.

"Are you scared, cousin?" he asks with a laugh. The offer is no longer on the table.

"Afraid of what? An overgrown crow with an even larger ego? I think not," I say with indifference. Any hope he had of keeping his life is gone. Now I want to end this—quickly.

"Do you need an invitation then, cousin? Or, is there some other reason you are taking this long?" He smiles and then he winks at me.

I will rip the offending eye out with my bare hands for that.

Without waiting a single second longer, I charge him, planning to kill him with my bare hands. The thought makes me smile as he begins charging me with a matching smile. Within seconds we collide in the middle of the clearing in a flurry of wings and arms, trying to break far enough apart to start swinging.

I underestimated my cousin. After hours of fighting, any strike I try to make either misses completely or glances off him. I had not thought I would need to use my speed this early in the fight, or even at all. His eyes flair when I begin to move faster and faster, laughing maniacally while he makes bigger movements around the space with no pattern. It's hard to guess where he will be next to be able to get one solid strike in.

I grow more frustrated with each hour that passes, while Kes seems to be having the time of his life. He's erratic, yet controlled, and exceedingly more capable than I gave him credit for. We block each other's fists while dodging any kicks; neither of us make any solid contact, until one of us grabs the other and we grapple for a while before breaking away. We have been repeating this pattern all night and I am unwillingly gaining respect for him. I think his aloof facade is just that, a way to make beings underestimate him. Begrudgingly, I find it impressive.

Second night rose several hours ago, and I am ready to end this. I take to the sky with the intent to confuse him with my speed, but with his element being air, he's easily able to maneuver in flight. I brandish my sword, hating being the first to pull, and he does the same. Somehow he still manages to wear a smile of pure delight as I dodge each swing and thrust he makes towards me.

Our swords collide, the sound consumed by the wide open sky, each of us applying the same amount of strength as we push against each other. It's the first time we have been remotely still the entire night.

"Having fun, cousin?" I ask him, seeing if I can break his concentration.

"The time of my life," he says, and I believe him. "What about you, cousin? Enjoying yourself yet?"

"Not particularly. I will admit, you are a well-matched opponent, however, I grow bored." I will never admit to feeling the beginnings of fatigue.

"What a shame… shall we try to kill each other now?" he asks, as if we have not been intent on killing the other since this started.

"I do think the time has come," I do my best to sound like Kes and then sigh dramatically, causing him to laugh hysterically. He still does not lose his focus.

"Oh, I do think you would benefit greatly from my influence. You are so…" he trails off, apparently unable to find a word to convey his thoughts. He mimes a ridiculous impression of me instead, and I cannot help cracking a smile.

"Unfortunately, we will never know how your influence might benefit me. I *am* about to kill you," I say, giving one last hard shove with my sword.

"We shall see about that, cousin. Before either of us are returned to the realm, I have one question I have wanted to know the answer to for a very long time."

My mind begins running through a list of things he could ask, it's never ending. "What is it you must know?" I am curious, however, it does not mean I will answer.

"What was it my father said to you before you sloppily removed his head?"

I am not sure why that was not at the top of my list of things Kes would want to know. I have to think about it for a few moments, I have done a wonderful job of pushing that stage of my life out of my memory. Kes looks at me expectantly, while I recall the memory.

"He said, 'This is not your fault, and you bear no responsibility. You do not deserve the father you were born to, and one day his control will end. You will make a fine king, nephew.'" We are both silent while Kes absorbs what I said, and I return the memory to the forgotten place in my mind.

"I barely remember him, and I must say, he could have said something a bit more dramatic. He was about to die, after all. Are you sure you are recalling it correctly?" I nod in response. "That is highly disappointing. Oh, well." He shrugs, surprising me with his reaction. I expected rage, not indifference.

With that, Kes slides just enough to the side as I continue to push into him causing me to jerk forward. He grabs me and attempts to pull his sword free, but his movement has given me the ability to crush his sword downward as I twist out of his grasp. I bring my sword up and send it arcing towards his head.

He gets his sword up just in time to block mine. His sword being made from an ordinary metal, and the combination of whatever this white metal is—moon blessed if Ulgridge is to be believed—with the speed and strength I put behind the blow, shatters his. I expect him to show a hint of fear without a weapon. I should have known better.

He laughs at the stump of the sword before chucking it over his shoulder and backing far enough away to give him a better range of movement. He windmills his arms in front of him before bringing them together horizontally and then throws his hand out. I move with my lighting fast speed and slice into each blade of air he throws at me.

What a clever trick.

When the full moon begins to rise once more and a new night begins, I know this will not be ending anytime soon.

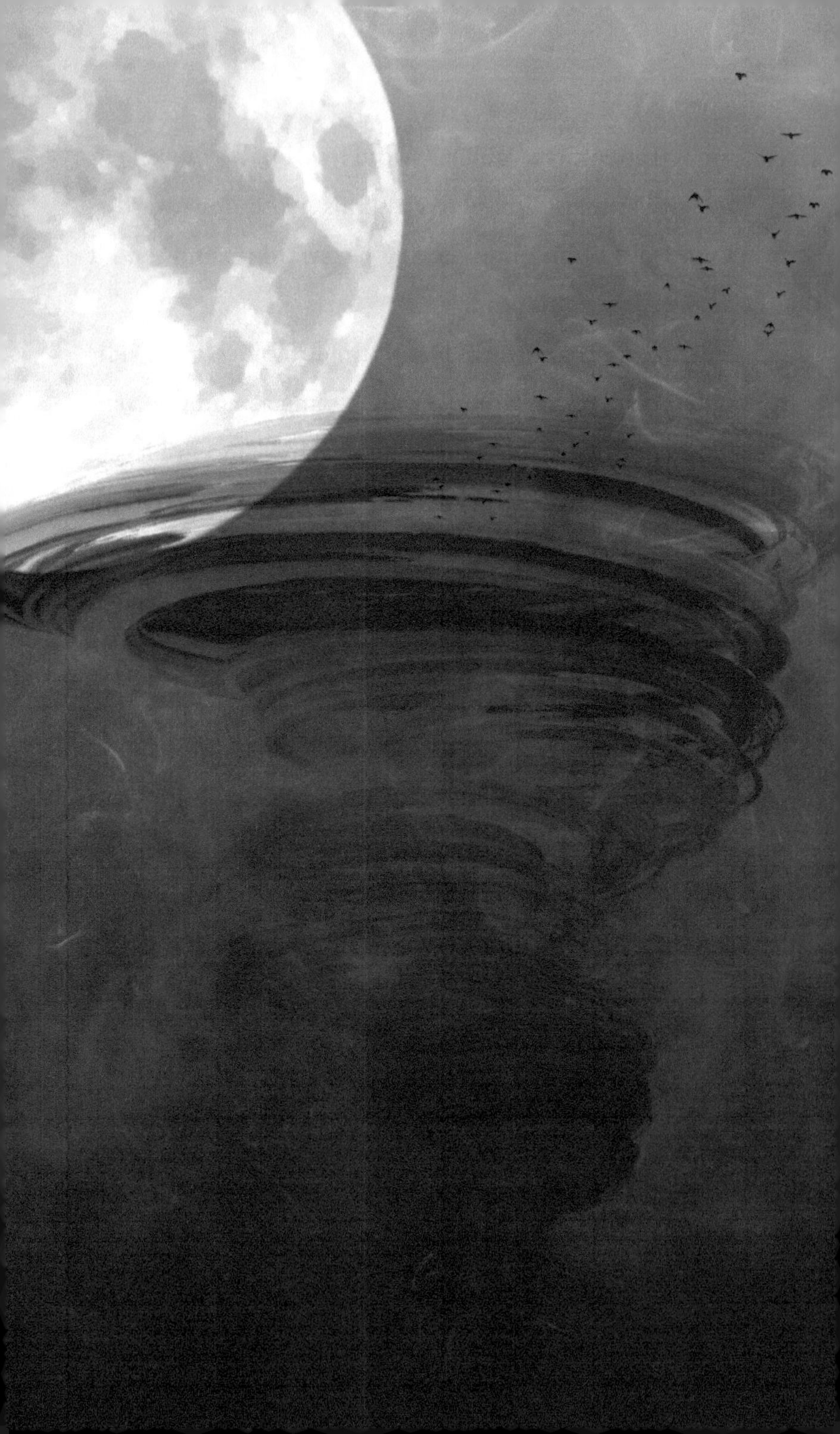

Eighteen

KES

The Final Round

This is becoming ridiculous, even for my standards. For the past five nights we have continued to fight—on the ground, in the air, with magic, and sometimes with new weapons we call to ourselves. The third day we spent most of the night porting around the clearing trying to catch one another. I found it rather enjoyable, but the remaining spectators did not, leaving us to go in search of something more entertaining.

We each dipped too close to the bottom of our wells and we were almost forced into sleep. Neither of us mentioned to the other how dangerously close we were to empty, and yet we quit porting at the same time. A silent agreement to allow our wells to replenish.

Now, the sixth first night is coming quickly, and while we still continue, both of us have slowed considerably.

Our bodies, our wings, our power, and even our magic is difficult to use. I can tell Ciaran feels the same as I do even though neither of us will ever admit we are exhausted.

Several nights ago, I thought this was a grand idea. I would beat Ciaran into a blue pulp and then walk away telling him I changed my mind and he could have the throne. When we crept into the second night, I was excited; it had been a long time since I was challenged like this. By the fourth night I was annoyed, and Ciaran? Well, he was mad in a *big* way.

The last two nights we both began moving slower and telegraphing our next moves. We finally started getting hits on each other. I managed to slice the side of his abdomen with a blade of air, and he managed to stab my wing with that ridiculous sword of his. Our bodies are having a hard time healing us with our power so depleted, making every punch we land leave bloody cuts and bruises behind.

First night comes for the sixth time. We both groan as another night has passed and we are *still* in the same damn clearing. At this point, we are waiting to see who will drop first, and it's not going to be me, that is for sure.

"Cousin, do you wish to admit defeat? You are looking rather worse for wear," I ask him, too tired to put any of my usual flair into my words.

"Am I? Strange. I could say the same about you," he says, even his words sound tired.

"You could end this now. All you have to do is say, 'Kes is the best prince in the entire realm,' and then we could each be asleep in our beds within moments." Ciaran barks out a laugh.

"Kes, you sound like you are the one begging for this to end. Perhaps you should be the one to proclaim me the best prince in the realm." I want to laugh, however, I am afraid if I start I will never stop.

"What do you say then—we give it everything we have until one or both of us is defeated?" I ask, no longer thinking it's possible for either of us to kill the other. It's a higher probability we end up knocking each other out at the same time.

"You do realize that is exactly what we have been doing for going on six nights now, right?" he asks, with a half-assed kick to my side. I do not think his foot made it even two feet off the ground.

"You call *that* giving it everything you have?" I taunt him.

"Just do not forget you were the one asking for it," he says with a sigh. He begins to gather his shadows to him as I get a whirlwind going. Right when I throw it, he tightens his shadows around him, providing protection from any damage the wind would have caused. I am not ashamed to say, that little trick never fails to impress me.

He pulls his sword and slashes at me in quick succession before attempting to bury his blade into my neck. He nicks me a few times; luckily, I am able to dodge the business end of his blade for the most part. Quicker than I expected, he makes me think he's coming for my neck again only to throw the blade with a surprising amount of force. It would have hit its mark, burying itself in my heart, had I not thrown up a shield of wind, knocking it away to land somewhere off in the distance.

I waste no time transforming my shield into spikes of air and shoot them all at him simultaneously. He has enough speed left, allowing him to miss most of them, while a few graze him, and one goes through his wing. Now, we each have a hole in our wing.

He comes at me with half the speed he had several nights ago, even so, he's still faster than me. I flap my wings and shoot up into the sky right as he runs through the spot I just vacated. Seconds later, he meets me in the air and we volley our elements back and forth at each other. Both of us remain mostly intact.

We fly toward each other at the same time; we could not have planned it better if we tried. The collision is the biggest impact either of us has taken in a few nights, catching us both off guard. Somehow our wings get tangled up and we start to free fall as we desperately attempt to disentangle ourselves. When we finally get our wings apart, we both try desperately to gain some traction, however, we are spinning too quickly for our wings to open fully. When they finally do, it does not matter, our wings are no longer strong enough to keep us in the air.

We spiral out of control, and the ground grows closer as we plummet. With my last bit of strength I throw as much wind under us as I can, slowing us down mildly. We crash together, hitting the ground hard. Groaning, we each roll onto our backs right next to each other.

Ciaran growls and mumbles something cranky under his breath. Even after nights of fighting, he still has the energy to be in a mood. He really needs to learn how to lighten up and have a little fun.

"You need to find yourself in the company of several females," I say, unmoving. He's quiet for so long I think he's not going to respond.

"What do you think I have been doing these past few months?" I turn my head and grin at him.

"You dog!" I gasp with false offense. We both grow quiet, until an idea strikes me.

"You know, I bet any of the females of the palace would jump at the chance to have us both, at the same time." He turns his head to look at me and raises a single eyebrow.

"That could be... educational," he says with all seriousness.

"After we sleep for an eternity, of course." I do not think I can even attempt to make it to my bed at this moment.

"Of course. After we sleep," he agrees. We lay there, side by side, staring up at the night sky saying nothing for several minutes.

"Kes?" Ciaran asks, breaking the silence.

"Yes, cousin?" I reply, curiously.

"You are fucking annoying," he says, as if it's a fact and not his opinion. I stare at him for a few moments before I howl with laughter. It does not take long for Ciaran to join me, laughing with such force we have tears streaming down our faces. I realize then, we will never be as close as we could have been once upon a time.

However, we will be just fine.

Acknowledgments

Almost one year ago, I sat down to write what would become my debut book, Prince of Darkness. I remember the elation I felt after finishing the first draft, and then again when I held my book in my hands for the very first time. What I did not know then and have since learned is all of that was the easy part. The hard part is after publication.

Being an indie author is a wild ride, one you can't do alone if you want to survive. You need support both at home and online. You have to build a community and fill it with family and friends who love you, fellow authors who get you, and the readers that inspire you to keep writing—demand it even. You need to surround yourself with people who will remind you daily that you ARE good enough and you CAN do it. I am lucky enough to have just that.

My parents, Dave and Lisa Thoma, along with my brother, sisters, nieces, and nephews, are unwavering in their support. They are the people who sacrifice time with me and do so encouragingly while I chase this dream. They are the ones who afford me the opportunity to spend as much time "authoring" as I do. They are the ones who love and support me unconditionally.

I call it "authoring" because it is so much more than writing. Overnight, you gain a multitude of jobs that I know I did not anticipate needing to do. Suddenly, you become a formatter, a designer, maybe even a cartographer—the hardest of them all, though, is becoming your own Director of Marketing and the dreaded social media manager. That's where your online community comes into play.

I am incredibly lucky to have met so many beautiful strangers from the online bookish community who have become amazing friends. People like Lona, who was the first person to hype me on Tiktok, and Amanda, who was the first person to fall in love with the world I created. Tia, who is always coming up with the funniest posts and pulling the best quotes from PoD (she's to thank for the quote on the back of this book). Jamie, who took me by the hand and deposited me into the Bookish Crew IG chat, and now I don't go a day without talking to those wonderful people.

Leah (and Amanda), who asked me to join the Facebook group The Queen's Library because they were reading PoD for their monthly bookclub and wanted to know if I would be willing to do a Q&A. I will never forget joining their group and having people be excited that I, a no name author, was there. I remember thinking, "If they only knew how quirky and chaotic I am." Needless to say, they do now, and for some crazy reason, they still love me. However, what they did not know was how encouraging and validating their excitement was and continues to be. That group is filled with some of the most incredibly kind women you could ever meet.

One of the most important things an author can have is a Street Team. The poor souls who signed up for mine deal with my chaotic "let's do all the things all the time" to my three to five business months of "now you see me, now you don't". There is no inbetween and for some reason they have not run away yet. Thankfully, Ashley is there to keep things consistent for the twenty five deep hype squad.

Another one of those "must haves" for authors are beta readers. These are the people you trust to see your manuscript first and then rip it apart—respectfully, of course. Jamie, Emily, Allie, and Amanda were all so different in the feedback they gave and the things they each paid attention to. The feedback was awesome, but more than anything, I loved the commentary. It was hilarious reading some of their "thoughts" on certain characters.

After the manuscript has transformed into a nearly finished novel, it gets passed to the editor, Kimmie Chonko. I am so beyond lucky to have a little "sister friend" who is willing to trade services—edits for hair. Silly goose, it's a win win for me. I get edits and quality time? Count me in!

However, before any of that can happen, it's just me, Scrivener, and Jess Bosworth in a crashing Google Doc. Jess is not only my "sister friend," she is also my alpha reader. She reads everything as I write and then reads it all 39924849337x more. At this point, I am not sure who has read PoD more between the two of us. She loves my characters and world so much that she nearly revolted when I said I was doing a rewrite on some of PoD. Luckily, it all passed the Jess test. I feel like she is always running behind me, picking up the things I drop along the way. Like chapter notes and Facebook groups. She has also given me a complex about the usage of the words "but" and "so," BUT I SO could not do this without her! (I have no idea how many but's and so's are in here, and I'm leaving every single one of them. HA!)

Some days the negative intrusive thoughts win, and while it is awesome to have the support of the ones who love you and the stories you tell, there is something about having people to talk to who get it. People who cry over the same things and deal with the same self doubt as you do. That is where your fellow authors come in clutch.

It's funny because there was recently some drama on Tiktok (when isn't there?) about authors being in competition with each other. However, that could not be further from the truth. We write these books, which take us anywhere from months to years to write, and our lovely readers consume them in a day. The group of authors I surround myself with share the same mindset, a rising tide lifts all boats. If even one indie author has success, it elevates the legitimacy of the community as a whole. We get just as excited for each other's wins as we do for our own.

We help each other with our dreaded blurbs (Ellie Lukas), and sometimes you come across a fellow author who will read your book, make a funny Tiktok about it, and then one day be inspired to completely rebrand you, make you truck loads of character art, and even design your COVERS for you! Rebekah Sinclair is not only one of the most talented individuals I have ever met, but she is also kind and giving. She is one of those people who naturally thinks about others and what she can do to help them. I keep trying to figure out what I bring to the friendship besides bird puns and chaos, but it's too late now. I told her all sales are final, and she's stuck with me for life!

Finally, that brings me to you, the reader. From arc readers to the reader who said "sure" on KU, if it were not for you, this would all be pointless. You take a chance on us, baby authors, and make it possible for us to keep going. Your reviews, no matter if they are critical, negative, or glowing, are important to not only the legitimacy of an author but also the growth of our skills. The mere fact that you chose to grace my words with your eyes and step into the world I created for a few hours is both terrifying and exhilarating.

What I am trying to say is that I am incredibly lucky. I have shared with you a small peek into the love and support that surround me every day. I often say I think my superpower is meeting the right people at the right time, and I think the incredible individuals around me are proof of that. I could never put into words how truly grateful I am for every single one of you. You will never understand the impact you have on my life and how validating you all are, and we know I am a whore for validation.

I'm not editing this, and I am sure it's filled with typos and a multitude of runon sentences, but this is just me raw dogging my gratitude for each of you. I know I am easily distracted, obsessive, stubborn, social, unsocial, talk super fast, and can be a lot, so thank you all for not only putting up with me but for loving me in spite of... well, me.

I love you all,
Amber

OH! HAPPY BIRTHDAY OLGA!

Hi! I'm Amber Thoma, the author of *Prince of Darkness* and *Heirs of Darkness*. I have been a reader for as long as I can remember. I blame personal-pan pizzas (IYKYK) for instilling an obsessive addiction to the many worlds books could take me to early in my life. I grew up in Northern Virginia and lived there until a few years ago, when I moved to a sleepy little college town in the mountains. I live in a 111 year old home with my dog, Lilith, and my cat, Kitten (very original, I know), and I am minutes from my family.

Like many people, lockdown made me reevaluate my life. For over a decade, I knew there was something I needed—a change. I played around with so many ideas. Like moving to a different country, going back to school, and starting a family. None of those felt right. The part of me screaming, "YOU'RE ON THE WRONG PATH," never silenced.

Listening to my intuition when the logical side of me was smashing the panic button was terrifying. That first step off the path was the most uncomfortable thing I had ever done. They say you have to get uncomfortable if you want to enact real change. Well, I got wildly uncomfortable and uprooted my entire life, and I will never stop being grateful for taking that first step.

If I had never taken that step, I would not have had a year of time with my niece before she suddenly passed away. I would never have taken the time to address my mental health. I definitely would never have sat down and written a book, and committing to a 5 series saga that will take me ten to fifteen years to complete would have completely overwhelmed me. I would have given up before I started, like I have so many times in the past. The folder of several dusty novel plans and intros can attest to that.

What is the moral of the story? Do not let fear keep you from taking that first step off the path you know you are not meant to be on. After all,

Fate gets what fate wants.